THE
DELILAH
CHRONICLES

Cover photo and book design by Leif Södergren

Special thanks to F.B. Leffew

ISBN 978-91-982015-3-6

LEMONGULCHBOOKS
www.lemongulchbooks.com

For
Angela

*

and for Keif,
he knows
why.

Also by
Donovan O'Malley

LEMON GULCH
Third Edition
of the Comic Cult Classic

**THE IMPORTANCE
OF HAVING SPUNK**
A Comic Novel with a twist
to the battle of the sexes,
and a nod to Oscar Wilde

OUR YANK
An American student
comes of age in Oxford during
the Cuban Missile Crisis of 1962

**THE FANTASTICAL MYSTERY
OF RITTERHOUSE FAY**
A London Tale

**WOMEN WHO LOVE
& OTHER STORIES**

THE JIMMY JONES SKANDAL
A humorous bedtime story
for grown-ups.
Illustrated by the author

THE DELILAH CHRONICLES

THE COMIC ADVENTURES OF
A 39-YEAR-OLD DIVORCÉE
DOING IT **HER WAY**

DONOVAN
O'MALLEY

LEMONGULCH**BOOKS**

CONTENTS

1

DELILAH SOBERS UP
AN OLDER LADY

Mum was deeply unhappy with Delilah's new life and didn't care who knew it. Delilah, who knew it and didn't care, girded her comely loins, coaxed her shabby, little MG Midget to life and with a screech of balding tires she and Mum were off to St. Pancras station. Mum, after an overnight with her daughter would now be deposited on her train to the suburbs.

But first, irresistible force must meet immovable object over morning tea and iced buns in the railway caf -- a fretful half-hour that had, since Delilah's divorce, become ritual.

"It was as big as Boadicea's horse's arse!"

"You're mixing your metaphors, Delilah!" said Mum who had recently begun evening-school poetry.

" I only wanted a shower blender, not a freaking space platform!"

"Keep your voice down, dear, the wide world is listening," cautioned Mum.

"When I politely asked the plumber to replace it with the one I'd ordered, the rude bastard spoke to me as though I hadn't a brain in my freaking head!"

Mum flushed, hoped no one had overheard her daughter's outburst and took a delicate sip of tea and nibbled daintily at her iced bun -- someone had to set a seemly example. Then, Mum, no angel, checked her watch, sighed and said "I loved that Jaguar your Trevor purchased whilst you were married. I was so proud when you brought me to St. Pancras in that Jaguar. You should have taken that Jaguar when you divorced him."

"I can repair the Midget myself, Mum."

"Women do not repair autos! Delilah. I'll make no secret of it. I do not care for that rat-like sportscar of yours."

"It's an MG Midget, Mum."

"It is not a Jaguar."

"It's a freaking Classic, Mum!"

"It's old! I am ashamed to be seen in it! We look like a pair of tarts on the prowl in that ancient vehicle of yours!"

Mum, who was incapable of not speaking her

mind, continued recklessly. "It has been a year," she moaned, "since you abandoned your loving husband."

This was Trevor speaking from afar. Her mother adored him, abhorred her. But Delilah, grinning, continued melodiously, "I am going to build a brick wall, darling."

"Ladies don't lay bricks!" snapped Mum, instantly.

"A brick wall so that Nigel's freaking dog cannot pee on my potted lilac."

Mum delicately sipped her tea, frowned and again glanced fearfully about. "Who on earth is Nigel?"

"The yobbo next door. He'd piss on it himself if he could. The S.O.B. probably has!"

"You've become coarse. Come to my evening poetry class!" pleaded Mum. "We're studying metaphors. I find them most relaxing. You are not comfortable in your single state."

"I think I'm going mad!" cried Delilah.

"So do I!" Mum pulled a hanky from her sleeve, dabbed an eye, swatted a tear. "Go back to him, love, take him by surprise before it's too late."

"Darling, I am happier than I have ever been. I have my very own little mews house."

"Trevor could have made a fortune on that derelict hut you call home! You ripped a fortune from that poor man's womb!"

Mum's poetry class did have its charms. "Darling, Trevor is not poor and my derelict hut, both floors of it, is about the size of your dining room table plus the kitchen sink. I spent more blood and treasure putting Trevor through business school than my hut is worth or may ever be worth." As cheerfully as possible, Delilah offered "I have my own business now, darling."

"There is no money in ceramic frogs and garden gnomes!" retorted Mum.

"Garden goddesses and smiling frogs. There's a qualitative difference."

"Your neighbour gentleman..."

"Nigel. He is no gentleman."

"He obviously hates you!" hissed Mum.

"It's mutual."

"Plumbers! Neighbours! Animals! You have this terrible trouble with men and their pets!"

"Drink your tea, darling, you'll be late for your train."

"You don't enjoy my little overnights very much, do you, Delilah?"

"Don't be silly, dear. I glory in them. Drink your tea." Delilah reached under their table and brought up a paper bag, pushed it across to Mum.

"What's this then?" said her mother.

"Prezzie for Mum."

Mum opened the bag slowly, suspiciously, pulled

out a pair of fine leather slippers, said "Are they new? Where's the shoebox?"

Joanna, a pretty woman in her late-twenties perched as gracefully as possible on a wooden crate in the plaster-dusted disaster that was Delilah's tiny kitchen to be, a work in progress that seemed to have no beginning or end. Delilah hunched on a pile of cement sacks beside her pretty next door neighbour. The contrast between the two women was of beauty-and-the-beast dimensions; overnights with Mum often required at least a day's recovery before Delilah's shell-shocked appearance inched back to its comely, thirty-nine-year-old-normal.

Behind the two women, twisted plumbing and wayward wiring protruded from the skeletal remains of several walls that required deft manoeuvres to pass among. Over all had settled the fine whitish dust born of the dismantling or disintegrating of almost everything. The stubborn insistence of wind through numerous draughty gaps kept the whitish dust in constant though fortunately subtle flux. But most worrying was the serious subsidence of the foundation, and the tilting, rotting floors.

All the small houses in this cobbled alley or mews, were once the stables and servant's quarters of the grand homes of the rich that lay just beyond a vast, overgrown garden expanse between them. Now, nearly a hundred years later, Delilah's little 'stable' was fighting to survive. She knew it must be rescued sooner than soon, and by her alone. She knew how to hold a saw and handle a screwdriver -- not the alcoholic, liquid kind -- that was her ex-husband's forte. Trevor, an investor, not a handyman, hadn't a clue how to properly drive a nail. Did you hear that, Mum?! Delilah could see, even now, Mum's scowl floating in the dust of Delilah's kitchen-to-be. How did that saying go? 'Keep your friends close and your Mum as far away as possible?'

Delilah, was ready, willing and desperately able but skint, and had hardly enough for the crucial clay and glaze that made her pottery possible -- and wouldn't till she'd begun to sell considerably more than she had. But hell's ballocks! Her heart suddenly jumped a beat then stopped for the briefest moment. Would there ever be a mate to share her new life?

Delilah the new optimist now shifted into high gear. Of course there would! and there he was, smiling in her head, this amiable, possibly prematurely balding, fit for his age, youngish man, just coming over the horizon on the up-escalator. His good sense visible even from where she sat on her cement sacks. He was fresh-scrubbed, fragrant, had a violin case on one hand and a bouquet of flowers in the other. And he wasn't the only one! Then, darkest doubt: How could two, fully-grown humans survive in this tiny space when it was problematic even for one?

Delilah was an optimist in many, many ways. But was she prepared for every eventuality? YES! When her aging charms failed, alone or not, she had her mews house to fall back on. Diamonds may once have been a girl's best friend but mews houses were the new forever! This was the straight scoop from her unique woman within. How could it fail? She ditched dark doubt and levered her comely frame -- these freaking cement sacks were hard! -- and hurtled back to reality. Had pretty Joanna just spoken?

No. It seemed not. Joanna was still unnaturally silent, puzzling over something. As always with Jo, it had to be momentous. Everything, mused Delilah, was momentous before the terrifying age of thirty. And after thirty, to the under-thirty, life was simply unthinkable! But after forty loomed the terrifying Black Hole! Astronomy had nothing on women. Women over forty had long experienced the icy nothingness, the remorseless abyss that was only now being revealed by science. By *men* of science, of course.

The two silent women, one young, the other, of a certain age, gazed thoughtfully out the open kitchen door into Delilah's tiny garden. It was a balmy afternoon and a faint breeze spun plaster dust round their bare ankles. Just visible outside was Delilah's pride, her potted lilac, too often the object of Nigel's loathsome rat-dog's cocked hind leg.

Suddenly Joanna, after four minutes of solitude, spoke. "Darren's bringing his kid," she sighed.

The kettle whistled. Responsible Delilah leapt to prepare tea.

"A boy, I think. He's four, I think. Not sure I can cope," said Joanna.

"Not sure I'd try," replied Delilah, blowing the usual dust from two chipped cups. All of her fine china was in storage with the furniture -- what there was of it.

"You'd try soon enough if you were in love."

"Oh, God yes!" cried Delilah and batted her eyes faux-fetchingly.

"See?" cheered Joanna, completely taken in, "Didn't I tell you? Oh, Delilah, it's the real thing for me this time." Joanna folded her hands on her stomach, said with a frightened smile. "I can feel it in here."

"I'd get an abortion."

"That's not what I meant. I'm serious. Darren and I, we're going to give it a six month's trial period. To see if he can cope."

Delilah handed Joanna a cup of tea, sat again on

the pile of cement sacks. "So he brings his kid and a suitcase of dirty laundry and moves in with you for six months to see if he can cope?"

"Well, he can't stay with his wife, can he?"

"Why not? They're married, aren't they?" said Delilah, not greatly in the mood for chit-chat after an unusually tiring day in her garage slash pottery slash ceramic frogs and pigs factory. She hadn't yet had the time and absolutely not the money to attend to all the necessaries the house urgently required. Like the dreaded subsidence. Terrifying! She had been told total collapse was not out of the question. A shudder shook a drop of tea from her cup.

"Well, his wife doesn't like him, does she?" replied Joanna. "How can you live with a person who actually doesn't like you?"

"Try not marrying them in the first place," said Delilah and winced as her own ten year marriage reeled by in her head. Joanna shot a soul-shaking, under-thirty smile to cheer her and took a sip of tea. Delilah easily saw why Darren was moving in for a trial period. What man could resist? If she had Joanna's looks she would move mountains. Then, just for fun, move them right back again.

"I think Darren will cope. I hope I can. It's lovely, for a change, being loved by someone who loves you. Helps you cope," said Joanna.

"I'm certain it's a basic requirement but I'm sure I wouldn't know."

"Trevor loved you, didn't he?"

Delilah winced again, rolled her eyes and was silent. She dropped an extra sugar into her tea to compensate for a sudden hollowness in her stomach. It wasn't often she felt this way. Her innate optimism forbade it. But her pottery wasn't selling and her house was subsiding and she pictured herself sinking into the muck with it.

Joanna pondered for a moment, managed "Oh, sweetie, couldn't you cope?"

Delilah looked up, threw off the gloom and smiled cheerfully, "Nope."

After Joanna had gone, Delilah rose, meaning to water her potted lilac when Nigel's back door was flung open and his detestable little dog sprang forth. Nigel watched, scratching the exposed hairy belly beneath his dingy string vest and grinned as the little dog dashed directly to Delilah's lilac, cocked its leg and peed. Delilah stormed out of her kitchen but stopped dead when the little dog bared its tiny teeth and growled ominously, far louder than any little dog should have. Delilah immediately retreated -- the horrid little monster might be rabid. She put nothing past Nigel. "Your dog has just pissed on my potted lilac!"

"It's Nature's way, 'n' it, darlin'?" said Nigel, grinning still.

"I demand you keep your dog out of my garden!"

"Sa matter, darlin'? Can't cope? Havin' trouble copin'?"

Delilah slammed back into her kitchen and its ruinous riot of wires and pipes. "Eavesdropping yobbo bastard!" she wailed into a small puff of plaster dust.

Almost immediately from just beyond her front door came a great and strange, ripping crash. A noise like no other! Was her tiny home, as officially predicted, in a sudden state of collapse?! Would she, it, and her new life be sucked into a whirlpool of wreckage never to be seen again? Not even by her ubiquitous mother? Am I being punished for desiring something too much? Was God really a man after all? Hell's total ballocks! These were Delilah's exact thoughts, all lumped into the split-second before her hand grasped the doorknob and she sprang out to 'safety', fearing the worst.

And there it was! Not quite, but almost. Embedded to the hips in the shabby canvas top of her Midget was a drunk, dishevelled but well-dressed, and once superbly coiffed woman in her late sixties. This weaving woman stood for a moment glaring at Delilah then slipped slowly through savaged canvas into the car seat below and began to snore.

"You can't stay there!" cried Delilah who'd had quite enough already with the Yob and his dog. The woman snored on. So Delilah threw open the car door and gently prodded her. "Why are you in my Midget?!"

The snoring ceased, one eye opened. "Wha'?" was mumbled.

"Why are you in my car?" repeated Delilah, pronouncing each word slowly, kindly, but distinctly.

"Shilling," muttered the woman, blinking open her other eye.

"What?"

"Shilling, you silly cow!" slurred this mysterious, well-heeled, very drunken woman.

Delilah grabbed one of the woman's arms and pulled. "I command you to remove yourself from my car! You'll be sick in it!"

"Right you are," the woman slurred, then promptly vomited and passed out again just as Joanna thrust her head from her upstairs window.

"Delilah! Darren is trying to sleep! He had a busy night. Could you keep your guests quiet, love?"

"This woman is not my guest!"

Joanna stuck on her glasses and took a long look. "What woman?! I can't see any woman."

"She has lodged herself in my car and vomited."

"Couldn't she cope?!" called Joanna who craned her neck for a better look.

"Apparently not! Help me get her into the house before she vomits again. For chrissake, Jo, move it! Help me!"

An hour later Delilah, with a tray of coffee and toast, stood knocking at her own bedroom door. There was no answer. She knocked again and tried the door. It was locked. "Phyllis? Phyllis? That is your name? I heard you moving about. I've brought coffee and toast. You must be hungry. Please, Phyllis, open the door."

After a moment, from behind the door: "No."

"No?!" Delilah was astonished.

"No!"

"Might I courteously remind you that you are in *my* bed in *my* bedroom?"

"Might I courteously remind you that you are being far too familiar for a total stranger? And *your* bedroom is a mess."

"I know it's a mess but it is my mess, not yours. Did you know that you have also destroyed the top on my car and vomited in it?"

"That was a car I vomited in? I thought it was a wheelbarrow. What can I say?"

"You can say you are very, very sorry."

"I am very, very sorry," slurred the voice beyond

the door.

"Now open this door."

"No. If I open the door you'll send me home," continued Phyllis from behind the door, "I do not wish to go home. Why did you address me as Phyllis?"

"It was on your driver's license in your bag."

"I don't drive."

"You lie. Your photo is on the license, Phyllis."

"If you look carefully, Ms busybody, you'll see that the license has been revoked due to driving whilst under the influence."

"Why am I not surprised? Open this door at once!"

"No!"

"Phyllis. You go too far!" announced Delilah.

The door inched open and Phyllis, in Delilah's much too small, much too old, chenille bathrobe, curtsied and swayed dangerously. Delilah decided at once that her uninvited guest was not yet sober. She motioned to Phyllis who obediently lurched back to bed. Delilah handed her a coffee. Phyllis took a swallow, glowered, said "Your coffee leaves much to be desired."

Delilah thrust a slice of toast at her. "So does my toast. You look like you've not been home for days."

"Three."

"Aren't they worried about you?"

"And who might they be?"

"Your family."

"Haven't any," she said and, one eyelid stuck shut, belched.

"Then who are all those photos in your bag?"

"You are a snoop!"

"There was quite a lot of money there too."

"I robbed a bank."

"You could have lost it."

"It wouldn't be the first time. Take it! Take it all, buy a new top for your jalopy."

"I might take you up on that."

"I hope you do. In your fussy, prissy way. You're rather nice."

"I wish I could say the same."

"Really? Why?"

"Phyllis. How did this happen? How did you end up in my car?"

"Wasn't it obvious?! I was climbing your blooming house!"

"Why?"

"Jesus H. Christ! You are the most curious woman I have ever met!"

"Under the circumstances..."

Suddenly Phyllis began to sob.

"Hey! Stop that!" said Delilah, fighting her own

pre-sob snort.

"I was looking for a bloody old shilling! If it's still there," sobbed Phyllis. "It's probably gone! Gone, like everything else in this bleeding world! Please don't make me go home! I can't go home today! I can't!"

"Don't cry, goddamn it! I can't bear it when people cry! Especially total strangers."

Delilah too, sentimental sap that she was, snorted and began to cry, sat on the bed beside Phyllis, blubbing, letting it all out. She could never have let Mum see this loss of composure. Mum would completely misunderstand, think Delilah was crying for the lack of Trevor, the lack of what was to Mum, the basic married situation where all was well and frequently visited restaurants had white, initialled table napkins and knives and forks that matched.

Phyllis sobbed too, in great, gasping sobs that Delilah would never have allowed herself in company. She took Delilah's hand. "Let me stay here tonight, dear. I'll go tomorrow. I'll sleep on the floor. I've slept on floors before. Too many floors before."

"Delilah?! Delilah?! Are you all right?!" called Joanna from beneath the bedroom window.

"Piss off, Jo!"

"Are you all right?!"

"Yes, goddamn it!"

"You don't sound all right! Is that Phyllis woman

all right?"

"Jesus H. Christ!" sobbed Phyllis, "I've stumbled into a nest of spies!"

"Yes! She's all right too!"

"I am not, goddamit it!" protested Phyllis from her pillow.

"Delilah!" shouted Joanna, "Delilah, can you cope?!"

"Yes! I can cope! Of course I can cope! Have you ever known me not to freaking cope?!"

"Good! I'm taking Darren out to dinner and we want you to baby-sit little Mikie. It was Darren's idea. Darren is dying to meet you."

"Darren is dying to meet me? Ah, the stuff that dreams are made of!" Delilah had staunched her tears and was searching for a paper towel to wipe her eyes. "Sure, love, I'll take the kid."

Phyllis began softly to snore. Delilah, still wiping away at her teary face, laughed.

"You're a treasure!" called Joanna from below.

These were the first kind words she'd had today and a great lump throbbed in Delilah's throat. "Goddamn it, woman," she mumbled to herself, "get a freaking grip."

"See you about seven -- kiss!" called Joanna.

Several hours later, Mikie was sleeping upstairs

and Delilah was scrubbing away at Phyllis's now only vaguely sick-smelling but once miraculous coiffure. The cost of which, Delilah knew, might have bought all the bricks she needed for her garden wall. Or a new top for the Midget? Phyllis, sudsy and sober, said "You do me a world of good, Delilah."

Delilah glowed. Those were kind words number two. Things were looking up. But Phyllis had not again mentioned paying for a new car top. Would she remember? Mum hated Delilah's Midget already. Now, it was nearly roofless. Another problem to solve. With sticky tape. Delilah was good at that. Or was she? She'd ask her unique woman within. But at the moment, her unique woman seemed to be on holiday. Where did women-within go on their vacs?

"You never took down Jimmy's Auto Repair sign on your garage," said Phyllis as Delilah briskly washed her hair. "His sign is still there. I thought if I opened your door he'd be there too. But of course he couldn't be. He's dead. Why didn't you take down his sign when you moved in? This is a residence now, not a business. If it were a business it wouldn't be car repair."

"Why not car repair?" Delilah rinsed Phyllis's hair with her potted lilac's watering can and began to comb out the tangles. "I repair my Midget when it needs it."

"Jesus! You do? Ouch! You're pulling!"

"Why shouldn't a woman repair her own car?" snapped Delilah, giving Phyllis's wet hair a tiny, wicked tug, "I have as much right to repair my car as you have getting sozzled and falling through its freaking top." She said this clearly and, she hoped, suggestively. "Anyway, it is a business. Pottery. I do pottery and Garden Goddesses. And smiling frogs, and curly-tailed pigs."

"Of course you do, dear, sorry. I am sure you can do absolutely everything. And shall."

"I never took down that car repair sign because it's safer if it looks like a man lives here. Pretty kettle of fish, that. Revolting, isn't it? Puke-making. Women, alone, are targets. Or didn't you know?"

"God, how I know," laughed Phyllis, "I once had a sobering experience with which I shall now charm you shitless." She chuckled and sat up and shook the damp hair straggling over her eyes and crossed her majestic legs. "After my centuries-ago divorce I was travelling in Greece, forgetting. Or was it remembering? I'd been there on my honeymoon many years before. I was in Athens and a handsome, dark-ish, youngish Greek I met at my hotel bar proved friendly. He asked me out for a meal. I paid, of course -- he suddenly recalled he'd lost his wallet just that evening." Phyllis laughed again. "You know the sort of man I mean."

"Their number is legion," said Delilah who couldn't agree more -- Mum had recently supplied the unusual 'legion' from a poetry evening and it was more than appropriate.

"After dinner and six too many drinks," continued Phyllis, "we went for a walk, this Greek gentleman and I, under an obscenely bright, Athens moon. Throwing caution to the gentle breeze, I went to bed with him -- my hotel room of course. After we had... enjoyed ourselves and he had taken a long hot bath, he got a small box from his attaché. Ah! thought I. His little gift of gratitude for my aging favours. But nay! He tried, with a straight face, a perfectly straight face, to sell me a soap carving of the Parthenon. I wasn't buying. Even when he offered me an after-midnight discount." She sighed, then laughed. "At least his services were free!"

"There is comfort in that," said Delilah, laughing.

Phyllis groaned and nodded, replied "Is there? Darling, I live and I fuck and I fuck, but I never fucking learn."

"Why were you climbing my house?" Delilah, ever practical, was going to get to the bottom of this.

"Jimmy. Of Jimmy's Auto Repair. I saw his name in my local paper three days ago. The obituary -- I haunt the obituaries. I haven't been sober since. Not that this is unusual pour moi but..."

"How long since you'd seen him?

"Thirty years? More?" Phyllis tilted her head, searched the ceiling thinking. I saw his name and I thought of the shilling we'd hidden. At the height of our passion, hidden over your window. Your car seemed an excellent ladder. I was attempting to reach the shilling when..."

"I have never felt that way about any man."

"Are you a lesbian?"

"Not that I know of, though I'm sure it has its charms. No, I like men that way -- their bodies. It's their minds I can't freaking abide. It's a dilemma."

"I should say so."

"I'm divorced. Trevor, my ex, is English."

"And you're American?"

"Only half. Mum's English, Dad was Irish American, a champion boxer. He's dead. I was raised in California, married an Englishman, moved here, was married for ten years, got this place in the divorce settlement a year ago. So here I am, reduced to putting pans under my sieve-like roof and shooing pissing dogs away from a pitiful potted lilac."

"Surely it's not as bad as all that?"

"Of course not, I love being on my own. You're divorced, you said. From Jimmy?"

"No, dear. Jimmy was my first love. We never

married. It was sweet while it lasted but I didn't fancy wasting my life with a loser. He bet on everything from horses and hounds to decorative douche bags. Jimmy was a loser."

"Trevor wasn't. Everything Trevor touched turned to gold. Everything but me." Delilah laid down the comb, found a towel, shook it, tossed it to Phyllis who began to dry her hair.

"And?" asked Phyllis.

"I didn't exist on my own. I was simply an appendage of Trevor's."

"Like his willie?"

"Yes! But Trevor took better care of his willie than he did of me."

"Took it to all the nicest places, did he?" laughed Phyllis.

"Oui! Certainement!"

The women laughed together, felt comfortable with one another. Delilah longed to confide, to laugh so freely with her mother. Phyllis would have been only a bit younger than Mum but she and Mum were planets apart. Mum was, ultimately, the cosy past. Phyllis was the perilous future.

Delilah perched at the top of a small stepladder, stretched to reach the ledge over her window. "I've found the coin!" she cried.

"Shhh! You'll wake Mikie," whispered Phyllis. "Is it a shilling?"

"Let me hold it in the light." Delilah descended the ladder, said "Yes."

"That's it!"

Delilah handed the shilling to Phyllis who studied it, sighed and looked away.

"Sorry I didn't come round when Jo brought Mikie," said Darren. He and Joanna had come for his son. "I was soaking in a nice, hot tub."

"I thought you might be," said Delilah, and grinned ever so shyly, her irony visible for miles.

"Has Mikie behaved himself?" said Joanna quickly, anxious to avoid what she knew was coming, and adding "Could you cope?"

"Oh yes, love, I gave him a couple of sleeping pills. He's upstairs. He's slept like a baby. Which, of course, he is. In fact, we can't seem to wake up the dear little tyke."

Darren went white and bolted for the stairs.

"She's joking, darling!" said Joanna. She grabbed Darren's arm and with a forced, but utterly enchanting smile, pulled him back. "Delilah is our mews comedian. She keeps us in stitches."

"Darren, I'd like you to meet an old friend!" exclaimed Delilah, and led him deeper into the rubble of her home.

"She needs a man around here," he whispered to Joanna who gave him a loving look. But Delilah had overheard and silently pushed a roll of electrical wiring into Darren's path over which he tripped and found himself at the knees of the now quite attractive, tweaked and brushed, wine-glassed Phyllis, elegant on the scuffed leather chesterfield in Delilah's patchwork living room.

"Phyllis, meet Darren."

"Hello, Darren. I've heard a lot about you," said Phyllis, expertly sizing him up.

Darren pulled himself from the floor, said with a perfectly straight face "I hope it was all good."

To which Phyllis immediately replied, "actually, dear, it wasn't at all. Delilah says..."

"Darren's an engineer!" said Joanna quickly. "He designs big projects. Don't you, darling?"

"Uh-huh. Occasionally."

"Can you design a brick wall, Darren? I need a brick wall, love, desperately."

"Oh Delilah! Darren designs only big projects!"

"But can he do the important things, like dishes?" replied Delilah.

"I could if I tried," said Darren.

Delilah led Darren by the hand into the kitchen to a large pile of dishes and pots and pans.

"Big project. Try, Darren. Try."

To Delilah's surprise, Darren, in forty-five minutes had washed the dishes, swept the floor, scrubbed the front of the cooker and fridge and made them all a cup of very late, very nice, tea. Delilah could never hold a grudge, especially with someone she'd known for under an hour. Credit where credit was due. Darren had inadvertently made a friend. Of sorts. How was Delilah to know that before moving in, Darren, the big-time engineer had a part-time job as kitchen help which he was more than happy to relinquish whilst he learned to cope with pretty Joanna.

Phyllis lingered over a photo of Trevor as she perused Delilah's photo album at morning coffee. "I wouldn't kick him out of bed."

"Many didn't," replied Delilah.

"Trevor was a dish," said Phyllis.

"If you like fast food," added Delilah.

"On and off in a trice, was he? I may be shameless, dear, but I, for one, wouldn't have minded a bit of his hot sauce in my taco."

"Then you'd be one of too many."

"Not a chance," laughed Phyllis. "I'm sixty plus."

"Age posed no obstacle for Trevor."

"Ah, a man after my own heart."

"If it lay between your legs, Phyllis, then perhaps. Trevor's knowledge of anatomy left much to be desired. I mean that in many ways."

"Sorry, love," replied Phyllis, "I'm so accustomed to not being choosy that I'm not very choosy. Bless me, I'm a somewhat over-aged nymphet."

Delilah had never discussed Trevor in this intimate way, not even with close friends, but it was oddly easy with unshockable Phyllis who seemed to draw everything out. "Not to worry, love," sighed Delilah. "Best thing that ever happened, the divorce. I'm realizing my full potential only now. A woman must be utterly on her own to realize her full potential."

"Yes, dear," said Phyllis, "whatever that means."

"Whatever it is, most men hate it. They hate to see a woman doing things they believe only men can do," said Delilah. "It's all hush-hush and they won't admit it but they hate it with every freaking fibre of their being."

"Things like you repairing your car? Oh, damn! your poor top. I must make a-mends, if you'll pardon my pun."

"It had a hole already. Mum put her fist right through it. She said she was swatting a fly. But you don't swat a fly with a clenched fist. My Midget is Mum's surrogate for me. She pounds the hell out of us. It was a hopeless case long before you landed on it. Forget it."

"I never forget a debt of honour, darling. Anyhow, I'm hideously wealthy. You'll have a check in the post or the rest of the plunder you discovered in my sick-soaked bag. If you can bear the stench."

"Phyllis, my needs are simple. I am going to build a brick wall around my garden to keep the pissing dog next door away from my lilac. It'll kill its Yobbo owner to see me making a power statement. Doing it all by myself."

"Do you know how to build a brick wall?"

"Of course not. I can learn. If a man can do it, I bloody can."

"Do you really hate men so very much, dear?"

"*Do* I?" Delilah was surprised, no, gob-stopped. She'd never thought of it quite that way. She knew only how she felt this minute. Or when Mum, completely ignorant of the whole story, praised Trevor -- those minutes too. Mum always took the man's side. The side of the protector, the provider-man, the giver of gifts when their silent women behaved themselves. All the other bullshit that...

"They do not seem to be your favourite animal," said Phyllis, fracturing Delilah's rancorous contemplations. "Speaking of which..." Phyllis gestured toward the glass kitchen door, the only major improvement Delilah had yet managed.

Nigel's vile little dog had now approached her lilac. Delilah leapt up, rushed to the door, threw it open and stamped her foot. "Get the fuck out of here! You little runt!!"

The dog again bared its tiny, sharp teeth, held its ground and growled horrifically. Delilah slammed the door and sat with a painful thud on the rock-hard sack of cement, helplessly glaring out as the horrid creature gleefully peed on her lilac. Nigel, leering, opened his door, let in the dog and gloating over Delilah's glare, disappeared.

"I don't hate men, Phyllis. Only men like that. I don't hate Trevor. I was no better for him than he was for me. It just took ten years, fortunately without offspring, to know it. Jesus! I'm desperate for intimate male companionship. But it's got to be me who decides that I want him. I won't stand in a queue anymore waiting to be chosen by them. I've done that. I'm always chosen by the wrong bloke and everything misfires. "I ride the freaking escalators at John Lewis, scouring the landscape. I even have a plan. If I see a sweet, sensitive man I drop a package. If he picks it up -- I invite him for a pint. Simple as that."

But Delilah was also only too aware of the straying married man who, fresh-fucked and guilty, invariably ruined the rest of their evening. First with an agonizing admission of his married status followed by tearful tributes to his perfect wife who either did not understand him or did not deserve the likes of him. "The men I want," sighed Delilah, "have all gone somewhere else..."

"Where? Where have they gone? Tell me, darling, and I'll be there ASAP!" Phyllis laughed. "Where indeed?"

"You tell me," mused Delilah, "They must have escaped to another planet and been largely replaced by an army of yobbos who tap you on the shoulder and expect you to toss your tits in the air and fall panting into their hairy arms whilst simultaneously unzipping their beer-soaked flies for a pre-coital quickie." Delilah nodded toward Nigel's house across the tiny side garden. "Men like that."

"Methinks you've been wasting your time at the wrong watering holes, my dear."

"Sorry for the ridiculous outburst," replied Delilah. "Actually, I'm not as desperate as I sound." But her occasional physical need was no picnic and she felt she may have revealed too much of herself and become a bore. Was she like a freaking man in this respect? She'd consult her woman within when said returned. "Not," Delilah repeated, "Not nearly so desperate as all that."

"I am!" exclaimed Phyllis. "But then, lucky me, I've got the bottle for company. And a battery-powered little friend who knows me much, much better than I know myself."

They laughed again and Delilah's confidence returned. Phyllis might become the kind of friend Mum never was.

Delilah took several of Phyllis's own photos from the kitchen table.

"Your daughter's a knockout. How long has she been in the states?"

"Angela's been in California as long as I can remember."

"Your son. Where does he live?"

"Neil lives in Brussels. A company man. Like his cherished father."

"Where's his father now?"

"I should say I don't know and I don't care. I do. He married again a few years after our divorce. Happily, dammit! See what a selfish witch I've become? Whenever they're in London I pester the hell out of them. She's extremely nice, by that I mean patient, and they get on famously. I'm the only horror in their story."

"I won't disagree," said Delilah. "You've certainly got horror potential."

"I'd better go, sweetie," said Phyllis. "Your pottery awaits."

"I'll drive you, Phyllis."

"No, dear. It's not far. You've wasted enough of your precious time on me. I do assure you, it is a waste. Dozens have tried. Dozens have failed. You've done me a totally undeserved great deal of good. I thank you. Can I buy a vase or something? Are they for sale?"

"Thousands of 'em. I've got a freaking garage full. More than I know. Plus my more commercial line of curly-tailed pigs, and a shitload of smiling frogs."

"My smiling frogs never seem to become princes, love, and I had my fill of two-legged pigs long ago. So I'll give your commercial line a miss. But how about an excellent vase? Do you make vases?"

Phyllis perused a table of pottery and was impressed, said, "Jee-sus, these are superb!" Phyllis was pleased that her new friend should be so accomplished. She did not think it appropriate to mention she had once been a buyer of such things at Liberty's. It was a self she'd left many years behind. She paused, reflecting for a moment as she examined an especially fine vase and turned suddenly to Delilah. "I said I'd left Jimmy because I did not wish to spend my life comforting a loser. That was unfair. The tables finally turned. It is I who am the loser." She held up the colourful vase. "I love it. I absolutely love it, darling. How much? Break my bloody bank."

"A shilling."

Phyllis understood at once, found the special shilling in her change purse, placed it carefully in Delilah's palm and squeezed tight. "Why not? Can't say it's brought me luck. Maybe it'll change yours? Now, what have you got for a daughter in California and a son in Brussels?"

Phyllis moved cheerfully down the exhibit table in Delilah's née Jimmy's garage, setting aside one favourite pot after another.

Soon, Delilah and Phyllis, each laden with a box of pottery, marched the boxes into the boot of the Midget. With a screech, torn top flapping in the wind, they were off to Phyllis's.

"I don't want to open the door, darling. I do not wish to go in!" said Phyllis, the key trembling in her hand and Delilah hard by, balancing the two boxes of pottery.

"Open it!" cried Delilah, "I'm freaking falling over!"

Phyllis fumbled open the door and they entered.

"Phyllis, it's a palace!" Delilah was impressed, even shocked. She had not anticipated a showcase of perfect taste. It was precisely what Delilah would have chosen had she Phyllis's means. Or at least what Delilah thought she would have chosen. Life was hell when her woman within was unavailable and Delilah's opinion of herself occasionally slipped its leash.

Delilah carefully set the two boxes of pottery beside an intricately carved table at a corner of the oriental carpeted floor that seemed to go on forever.

"A woman comes in twice a week, tidies up," said Phyllis, "washes the glasses -- and there are a few -- polishes the...polishes the -- I hate it here."

Phyllis broke off and turned away. Delilah approached to comfort her. Phyllis motioned her back, took a thick wad of banknotes from a silver box on a small, highly polished table, handed it to Delilah, said "Your car top, darling."

"This is far too much," replied Delilah.

"For the pottery too, dear."

"But I gave it to you."

"It's your livelihood, love. For chrissake take it!" said Phyllis almost angrily. "You'd better go, dear. You've been wonderful but I've got a little problem which must be quickly attended to."

Phyllis went to an elaborate bar cabinet, poured a whisky, quaffed it, said "I won't even offer you one. Nobody sane drinks at this hour."

Delilah said, "I might."

"You've been so kind, darling. Let's not ruin it."

"Damn it! I want a drink! I freaking deserve a drink!"

Phyllis smiled, poured another whisky, handed it to Delilah, and pouring herself another, said "I call it 'going out on a limb'. I have a few -- more than a few. I test the bounds of the possible. Like climbing houses. Have you never felt like climbing a house?"

"I do it all the time. In my head. But I have yet to fall through the rotting roof of a shabby little sportscar," said Delilah with a forced grin.

Phyllis grinned back, took a long swallow from her glass and sighed "Really kind people like you try to 'help' me but they always end up hating me, or I, them. There's an excellent reason for a daughter in California and a son in Brussels -- at a secure distance from monster Mum."

Phyllis was feeling better. She grinned enchantingly and quaffed the rest of her second drink.

"Look, Phyllis, I know I could, we could..."

"Rubbish, but thank you, darling." Phyllis extended her hand. "Thank you, Delilah, from the bottom of my heart."

Phyllis went again to the bar and poured herself a tall whisky, and without facing Delilah, said, "Goodbye dear."

Delilah waited for Phyllis to turn to her but she didn't. Delilah set down her untouched drink, started for the door.

"Delilah?"

"Yes, love?"

"Happy Birthday to you! I saw the inscription in your photo album." Phyllis now faced Delilah and holding up her glass lit the room with a florid grin and proclaimed. "To your good health, darling," and turned away again.

"Thanks," said Delilah. Near the door she stopped, dropped on the fine, polished table most of the bank notes Phyllis had given her. But reconsidered, picked them all up, paused, reconsidered again and dropped just a few. Phyllis heard the door and waved over her shoulder. But Delilah had already closed it softly behind her and was gone.

At her bar Phyllis sipped the tall whiskey and dabbed absently at her running mascara. "What a day this has been, what a gay mood I'm in!" she sang. There was plenty of time to shower and fix her face and change clothes. The evening was young. She'd soon be on the town. She felt luckier without the 'lucky' shilling to haunt her. That diary was locked forever, and she'd thrown away the key.

The car-top flapping violently, balding tyres screeching, Delilah braked before her house and climbed out to find a small cat sitting on her doorstep. She picked it up, cuddled it.

"Well, happy birthday to me! Where did you

come from?"

In the kitchen Delilah set a bowl of milk on the floor and placed the cat beside it. As she tossed her jacket over a battered kitchen stool, the special shilling jumped from its pocket and rolled across the floor. She bent with a grunt, picked it up, kissed it and said "So far, so good!" and tucked the shilling into her jeans pocket. Picking up the lapping little cat and its bowl of milk, she set them down in the living room. "It's warmer here," she assured the cat.

Outside, Delilah climbed the stepladder and returned the shilling to its original place on the window ledge and climbed down. Stepladder under her arm, she fairly skipped into her house just as Nigel's dog came trotting around a corner of her little garden and sniffed itself directly to its potted lilac victim. The dog, which was about to cock its hind leg, stopped dead. Its beady eyes had caught the flutter of an irritable magpie just across the mews about to swoop for a dive-bombing -- the dog had also violated magpie nesting territory. The bird swooped and the dog leapt to shelter through Nigel's open door.

The special shilling, glistening from its window ledge in the fading light, seemed to be admirably performing its assigned task.

But no. Slinking out from Nigel's door again and

sniffing the air to be magpie-free, the creature crept towards its sad, little lilac target. The dog growled, scuffed the surrounding dirt with its tiny front paws, cocked its leg, peed, scuffed again, peed again. If dogs remembered such things, this would have been a memorable piss indeed. Nigel leered happily from his open door, the little dog shot back into the house and Delilah's two base villains retired.

Delilah had made herself a cup of tea and with her new cat friend purring happily in her lap was about to open a brochure, "Masonry for Dummies", donated by Joanna's Darren who, at the moment, did not seem all bad.

2

DELILAH AND MEN
WHO WANT ONE THING ONLY

Mum frowned and sighed conspicuously with each sweep of the comb through her windblown hair and sulkily ignored Delilah whose fault this hair disaster obviously was. After a tempestuous moment of more frowns, more sighs, she threw her comb and mirror into her bag and, avoiding Delilah's eye, sipped daintily at her morning tea and delicately nibbled her iced bun. As usual, roiling waves of it's your fault splashed across the caf table and broke upon Delilah's lap.

"Poor Mum," thought Delilah.

"Poor Mum," thought Mum.

"Mum. I'm sorry!"

Her mother, frowning still, looked away, peered longingly through the caf window at her train's departure platform and nibbled and sipped, pinky finger extended -- somebody had to set an example for her errant daughter!

"Mum. Please?"

"Disgraceful! I was nearly blown away! The wind could have sucked me out through that hole in your vehicle's top! I could have been sucked up, cast out and struck down! Like a dog in the street! Disgraceful!"

"Mum, I've tried to tape it closed but it keeps coming unstuck. There are just so many other things that are more important, love. I'll have it fixed just as soon as I can afford it."

"That's what you always say, Delilah. But you never will. You never will because you can't. You can't because you are a woman alone and a woman alone cannot, nor should, afford it. Go back to your husband and he will do the affording."

"Women can afford many things, dear. Women have their own businesses and some are CEO's of huge, thriving international companies."

"This does not include -- correct me if I'm wrong -- women who clothe themselves in rags." Mum eyed Delilah's patched jeans. "Or women who are CEO's of bloomin' garages in broken down commercial mewses!"

"Mum, *many* things can be afforded by women!"

"That's what men are for, Delilah, that is their raison d'être! Affording things. Like decent roofs for rotten little autos."

"The ripped car top is not my fault, Mum. I told you. Phyllis fell through it and was sick."

"That car ponged so, I thought *I* would be sick! What was the old hag doing, falling through the top of a stationary motor vehicle?"

"Phyllis was having a bad time, darling."

"I should say she was! That drunken, vomiting old tart falls through the top of your auto and all you can say is Phyllis was having a bad time, Mum! Oh, Delilah! Go back to Trevor. Make him marry you again. Go back to Trevor before he re-situates himself. Go back and get decent. Stop consorting with inebriated riff-raff. Joyce Grudden says that your Trevor has recently purchased and installed a Nordic Sauna Bath in his newly constructed luxury double garage. That Nordic Sauna Bath could be yours, Delilah. You could use a good, hot Nordic bath. You look grimy, my girl. Grimy, scruffy and ill kempt!"

"It's all that filth blowing in, Mum. Through a woman-sized hole in my Midget."

"No filth blows into your Trevor's Jaguar, Delilah."

"He is not my Trevor, Mum. Not now or... Oh forget it!" Delilah quickly forced a bright new smile.

"I'm reading a brochure Joanna's boyfriend gave me about how to lay bricks!"

"Women don't lay bricks!"

"This woman will!" said Delilah and her mind screamed God! am I my mother's keeper?! and answered, No! She's mine! I am thirty-nine years old and Mum has become my ex-husband's stand-in!

"I saw that brochure on your tatty sofa. Masonry for Idiots!" said her mother.

"No, darling, Masonry for Dummies."

"What's the difference? Furthermore, there I sat in your junk heap of an auto only minutes ago as you stole..."

"Requisitioned, Mummy dear, requisitioned a few bricks from an abandoned building site. It saves tax-payer's money. There are thousands of such sites with a few overflow bricks just begging to be requisitioned. One must be able to assimilate opportunities when they offer themselves."

"I'm surprised you haven't been arrested. Theft is theft whatever fancy name you choose to give it. A rose by any other name, Delilah, is still a rose. My daughter is a thief. A thief is a thief is a thief!" said Mum triumphantly and added "Gertrude Stein said that!"

"But a rosy thief, Mum?" chuckled her thieving daughter.

"And that's not all!" Mum's jaw now set resolutely. Her lips tightened across her teeth into a mean, red pencil-line as she took a very plump, paper envelope from her bag. Her eyes narrowed, glinted venomously and she handed the plump envelope to Delilah. "I took the liberty of removing this abomination from your premises!"

Delilah took the plump envelope which instantly burst open, releasing a mini-waterfall of condoms that scattered on the caf table. Mum stifled a shriek, shielded Delilah with her bag as, humiliated for all the wrong reasons and scarlet from her cheeks to her bare elbows, her daughter quickly gathered up the condoms. Flushed elbows still showing through her worn pullover, Delilah tucked the sinister contents back into the envelope and crammed it, plump again, into her own scuffed leather bag. Mum scanned the caf to see if anyone had witnessed this dire event. No one had. Mum set down her bag-shield, sighed with relief then hissed "It's immoral," into her daughter's ear.

"It's intelligent. And they were on sale," Delilah hissed back. "We live in dangerous times, darling. Which reminds me," she said grinning, and baiting her mother, "I'm going to John Lewis's for the day."

"The whole day?" asked Mum, calmer but simmering, " in a bleeding department store? Why the whole day?"

"A whole day at least. I've given myself a mini-holiday from my pottery." Delilah smiled mysteriously, mock-yawned and looked away.

"Your secrecy does not become you, my girl. I demand to know what will take you a whole day at John Lewis's department store! You've no money to speak of."

"Finding a man, of course. I'm restless as hell. I'm jumpy."

"You're shocking, that's what you are. I'm surprised you've not been had up by someone in authority for loitering with intentions."

"So am I." Delilah grinned ferociously, pulling a wild-eyed face.

Mum buried her outrage in a distinctly, unladylike bite of iced bun and, getting down to business, said, "Why John Lewis's? Why not Harrod's? Harrod's is where the real men shop. Men who are tall, dark and solvent. You could wear your old Burberry raincoat and look like you belonged. If you must be immoral, Delilah, go to Harrod's for your men."

Delilah cast a hopeless look at Mum who, mirror in hand, was again sighing and tidying her hair.

"See you next week, love! If you can bear it!" laughed Mum as they hurried to the departure platform. "I'm joking!" she added seriously.

As the train moved slowly away, Mum called from her compartment window. "I took the trouble of ringing Trevor and informed him that deep in your heart of hearts, Delilah, you love him and are considerin' returning to him." Then she was gone. Was her mother still joking?

But now, on with the day. The whole day. It was escalator time!

Wide-eyed, vulnerable but not innocent, not in that cute, cliché, mid-twentieth century way her mother adored, here was Delilah, freshly scrubbed, garbed and glistening, descending on a John Lewis escalator. What actually, she asked herself, was she doing here, single again, at the ripe old age of thirty-nine on a manhunt? She had fine pots to throw, smiling frogs and garden goddesses to cast, a whole tiny mews house to rebuild, a brick wall to lay, a recalcitrant mother to tame. Yet here she was on the down-escalator, primed for action with, according to her plan, a wrapped package to be accidentally jettisoned at the appropriate time.

Delilah had, only seconds before, set her sites on her completely ideal recipe, a prematurely balding man of about her age who was as freshly scrubbed and glistening as she. He stood on the floor below, carried the required, but not mandatory violin case and was queuing for the up-escalator. Her mission: She must find a way to barge in front of him and drop her wrapped package. According to plan, if he picked it up and politely handed it back to her and his left hand was not adorned with the dreaded wedding ring, she would know he was a man of taste and sensitivity, no department store Lothario he, no serial philanderer like... err herself? This was a moderately disturbing thought and caused the fine hairs at the back of her neck to tingle, calling for urgent consultation with her woman within. But there was no time! Delilah was a woman of action and consequences be damned! She must now quickly reach her prematurely balding prospect's floor and follow him on the up-escalator!

Suddenly, her eyes still wide but wearying from scanning the crowd on three earlier escalators, blinked wider still. There, at the foot of this escalator was an astonishingly cute... she hated that word when applied to woman but felt it an acutely acceptable adjective for men. Only, obviously, if they were indeed cute which he indeed was, astonishingly so. But far too young. He stood near her violin-carrier and even from this distance above she knew this far-too-young man was err... far too young, and even farther from her type. Delilah didn't rob cradles, at least not since she herself had occupied one. She would certainly avoid him. Still...

She scanned the scene below, saw that her balding, freshly scrubbed prospect was moving ever closer to the crowded up-escalator while her down-escalator was taking donkey's years to reach him on the floor below. Panicking, she inadvertently glanced again at the far too young man. Here was a possible back-up. But hell's ballocks! He wore a cowboy hat and that spelled trouble. She'd no intention of exploring the freaking O.K. Corral ever again. She'd had an experience with a phony cowboy before she'd married Trevor. If this far too young popinjay -- popinjay?! Where in freaking hell did that come from?! Mum's evening class poetry? If this child-man tried anything, Delilah would swat him away like a fruit-fly! Still...

As the shopping crowd ebbed Delilah saw that cowboy-hat was wearing a western style suede jacket with leather fringes at the sleeves. He had a backpack with a small American flag sewn on, and below it was stitched TOM. He was reading a map and oblivious to all around him. Rather charming that. But not for her. Her gaze jumped back to her musical prospect -- might he be First Violin in some distinguished orchestra? Sad, about his receding hairline. But surely no obstacle to the mature adult relationship that Delilah knew would be utterly impossible with 'Tom' and his cowboy hat and his fringed leather sleeves. Still... A boy in your hand was worth two in your bush. She couldn't resist a chortle. She too, was poetical, Mum.

Her escalator finally reached the floor below and Delilah leapt off in panicked pursuit of her musical, fresh-scrubbed prospect just as Tom dropped his map and swung round to grab it up. It was precisely then, as Delilah passed behind him in full pursuit of the violin-carrier, that Tom's backpack struck her broadside and she was catapulted into a lipstick display. From its tumbled wreckage she watched, cursing silently, as the sensitive, violin carrier disappeared and was lost forever on the up-escalator. Well, fuck it! Semi-dazed Delilah was now politely confronted by Tom and he blushingly offered a strong arm and she hadn't the strength to swat him away like a fruit-fly. "Still," She muttered, gazing into his lushly lashed sky-blues, "still..."

"Oh, like, wow! I'm sorry!" said Tom and grabbed Delilah at her armpits and hauled her roughly aloft. "Oh, Wow! Did I, like, hurt you?!" he said, but dropped his map again, swung quickly around to catch it again, and knocked Delilah back to the floor -- again. She had lost her balding First Violin but at least still clung to her strategic wrapped package so all, she thought with a glance at strapping Tom, was not lost. Delilah had proved herself a capable woman, perhaps not able to leap tall buildings at a single bound or avoid twirling backpacks. But she had been prepared for any eventuality and here he was, gleaming in his cowboy hat and leather-fringed sleeves. Her backpacked back-up! "O.K. Corral," she murmured, "here I come!"

The agitated store floor-manager now plunged toward them through waves of startled shoppers. Delilah, quick as a fox, sprang up from the lipstick littered floor, grabbed the perplexed young man's hand, shouted "We need a drink, sonny!" and ran him, two steps at a time down the next escalator to freedom. As they rushed up a side street toward a pub she knew of, the wrapped package skipped away from her and bounced twice on the pavement, Tom made not a move to retrieve it. Had he seen it? "Fuck it," she muttered. So the wrapped empty shoebox that had once contained Mum's new leather slippers, stayed where it lay, in the gutter. Never mind, she'd wrap another for next time. One had to be flexible.

Delilah and Tom, sat at a small round table, Tom's backpack and his cowboy hat atop it, were on a chair beside them. He took a large swallow from his pint of bitter and exhaled noisily and Delilah said "You needed that."

Tom said "Yeah. Thanks a lot," set down his glass and grinned adoringly at Delilah who quaffed the last of her own half-pint, slammed it on the table.

"Wowww! You're like, really something! Haven't I..." began Tom.

"...met me somewhere before? No, cowboy, you would have remembered me if you had."

"Where have you..."

"...been all my life? I've been married. Depending, of course, on how old you are. American?"

"Woww! How did you, like, know I was a American?"

"You're in Sherlock Holmes country, cowboy."

"Shirl who?" He was serious. "Who's she?"

"Forget it, dude, I'm American too. I was born in Chi." What had happened to her posh, plummy tones?!

"Chi?"

"Chicago. But my Mum never approved of me and my American Dad raised me and I'm old enough to be your... err. Tom, let's face it. I am thirty-two. An heiress. I inherited a house... well, more of a broken down shack here in London... Oh, forget it." Here she was, already lying through her teeth. But it was in a good cause -- self protection from this sombrero-topped child, this potential heartbreaker. Besides, men morphed instantly into pathological liars whenever they spoke to women. Why shouldn't she lie? Especially about her age? What's good for the goose is good for the...she studied Tom, err...gosling? Still...

Tom found a pipe in his backpack.

Delilah watched him steadily as he packed the pipe, lighted it. Perhaps he was different? No. It was impossible. His age made that so. He was not only wet behind his ears, he was double-drenched, and consequently utterly unreliable. Still. He was gawky, and astonishingly cute. About eighteen or nineteen? So she said without blinking, because what on God's freaking green earth could she say to this, this preternaturally attractive almost-babe in freaking arms? "You smoke a pipe, I see," she said regretting it at once. Why was she always brought down to their level? Was she simply horny? Or just out of touch? She landed on 'horny' -- the perfect answer, agreed her woman within.

Puffing on his pipe, Tom replied "Yeah, I do."

He was not a great conversationalist. Now that was out of the way! Still... his curly ginger hair was...

Delilah, again said the only thing at this muddled moment she could think of, "You'll get cancer of the lip in a minute."

"Wow! Like, will I?"

No. He was not a great conversationalist. But just now, neither, she concluded painfully, was she. "My granddad smoked a pipe," she ad-libbed feebly, "He got cancer of the lip and died before my dear mother was born." If Delilah had had scissors handy she'd have cut off her tongue.

"Like, wow!"

"Like, yeah!" she added. She was feeling relaxed in her good old Americanese.

After what seemed to be an awkwardly long time but wasn't, the two were surrounded by empty glasses -- the barman, clearly and typically, thought Delilah, was not efficient. "Another?" asked Delilah of this pseudo-cowboy who'd had two pints already, her own reputed limit. And she was paying. No, he'd had three or was it four? Who's counting, her head said and answered: I am and I'm not the Bank of England. She began to count the empty glasses when Tom said: "Yeah, sure, I'll have another, if you're still, like, payin'. I'm a little, like, short."

"You look quite tall to me," said Delilah. Tom, fell into gales of guffawing laughter over her dreadful pun and Delilah knew, as she had known all along, that this too-young cowboy had been, like, a grotesque mistake. Still...

"Yeah, I'm payin'" she muttered, searching through her scuffed but well designed leather bag as the ghost of Phyllis's Athenian freeloader played in her head. "At least I think I'm payin'." Tom's American accent was annoyingly catching, especially to the displaced semi-American she was. It came too naturally and was disquieting. Why was she so freaking impressionable and keen to please? How could she be so easily influenced by a man, not even a man, but a pretentious, not awfully bright boy? Strike that -- make that: stupid boy! Hell's ballocks! Was simple animal lust dismantling the unique woman within her? Where was her common freaking sense?!

Delilah overturned her scuffed leather bag. A couple of coins rolled on the table. She shook her bag harder, the plump envelope of condoms shot out and burst open like an over-anxious piñata. Delilah stared dully at the scattered condoms, Tom stared in wonder at the scattered condoms. Delilah stared at him, he stared at her, they stared at the condoms together. Mum, too, somehow loomed glaring over their shoulders at the condoms.

"Tom?"

"Huh?"

"Can you play a violin?"

"No."

That said, he picked up his pipe and puffed, still gazing at Delilah and looking so young it actually hurt in the pit of her stomach. What a predatory monster she'd become! Lust-led! She'd lost touch with the solid values that once made her human, that made life beautiful and worth living -- that bored her shitless.

"Still..." murmured Delilah, "still..."

"What?" said Tom, "Were you speakin' to me?"

"No, lovey," she said. "Don't worry your pretty head."

Delilah and Tom slept in Delilah's bed, impervious to the bland morning sun through windows that hadn't been washed since Jimmy's Auto Repair. The two sleepers lay comfortably unconscious to the jungle-world of Delilah's half-finished bedroom: clothes that hung like tree moss from every exposed nail on raw, planked walls, shoes that spilled like overripe fruit from cardboard boxes, and a naked light bulb hanging from a baffling foliage of frayed wires. Two fake furs on a door hook provided the absent jungle fauna. A veritable cornucopia of metaphors Mum might have said, and none of them mixed.

Tom woke, sat up suddenly, yawned loudly, got his bearings in this alien vegetation. He fondly noted the sleeping, older woman beside him, gave her a gentle prod, hollered "Good mornin', girl!"

Delilah, always a deep sleeper when middle-age permitted, woke, moaned, and turned away from Tom.

"Good mornin'!" he repeated.

Delilah turned again, moaned again.

"Wake up, sugar!" said Tom.

"Who the hell are you?" mumbled Delilah from behind closed lids.

"Tom!"

"Go away, Tom."

"What's your name then?"

Abruptly fully awakened, Delilah sat up. The sheets fell away. She caught them, pulled them up quickly, more from the cold than from modesty.

"Hell's ballocks! It's freaking freezing!" she cried, "where have you brought me?!" God! she thought, this poor child will think I'm mad, not joking. It's too early for joking, and far too late to be rising with the sun. Mum, who had resolutely appointed herself Delilah's protector now that Trevor was out of the picture, would be livid. More for being in bed at this late hour than because there was a man, a very much too young man, here beside Delilah. Delilah didn't even care for the boy. He wasn't her cuppa. Still...

How did she get herself into these things -- or rather, she thought, how did these things get into her? She couldn't resist a guffaw. A full hearted belly laugh followed. Tom, of course, was not a thing. But he had a thing, and his thing was a thing, and his thing did get into her. She laughed again, felt she was becoming happily ruthless, and laughed yet again.

"You brought me, sugar!" Tom who was delighted

that his 'thirty-two-year-old' was so cheerful so early in the morning -- he liked his women like that! "What's your name, girl? You never, like, told me your name."

Delilah rubbed her eyes, her head, attempted to get her bearings. Her joke was a false start, she knew. She wasn't quite awake. She was a slow waker-upper. Slow to sleep, slow to wake.

"It's freezing. Turn on the electric fire," she repeated.

Tom crawled to the foot of the bed, switched on the fire. Delilah sat staring, dazed with sleep. Tom sidled up, gave her a sexy nudge.

"Hi, good lookin'. Whatcha got cookin'?"

"Fuck off, cowboy!" Then softer, "hungry?"

"Yeah!" said Tom, saluting her, actually *saluting* her! "What time is it, woman?"

Delilah found her watch on the bedside table, said "ten o'clock. Want an egg?"

"Yeah!"

"Yeah what?"

"Yeah, please?"

"What kind of egg, cowboy?"

"A chicken egg?"

This annoyed Delilah. Was he being cute? Still... She seemed to be depending rather too much on her *stills* lately. But what the hell, "I mean how do you want it?"

"Huh?"

"Oh jee-sus," she mumbled, "it's going to be that kind of day."

"Huh?" said Tom.

"Boiled? Soft-boiled? Fried? Scrambled? Raw?"

Tom sprang happily out of bed, cried "I'll cook the eggs!"

Tom, in Delilah's flowery kimono, danced about her, teasing as she, her face still disfigured from sleep, huddled over a pan of frying eggs. He suddenly ripped off the kimono and, bare-arsed, went into a dramatic pose, smiling maniacally at dismal, disengaged Delilah who only wished to fry the freaking eggs and get rid of this child who now struck a pose, and shouted "I'm a famous statue! What famous statue am I?"

Delilah squinched her eyes and groaned.

"Huh?!" he persisted, arms over his head, pumping his perfectly respectable muscles, "Huh? What famous statue am I?!"

"The Statue of Liberty?" she managed.

"Nah!" cried Tom, happily. "Guess!"

"Please, cowboy, turn down the volume."

"Well?" he insisted, "what statue am I supposed to be?"

"Darling, that's the only American statue I know but I'm good on music. Ask me about music," she yawned. She'd had two piano lessons as a child -- her very first profound brush with Culture.

Tom maintained his pose. "I am The Dyin' Slave by Michelangelo, a famous I-talian. We studied him last year."

Ballocks! she thought, she'd once, as a student assistant, managed a whole year of Michelangelo and this over enthusiastic, almost terrifyingly vital boy looked more like Spartacus than any freaking dying slave! But she simply rammed a dish of fried eggs into Tom's stomach and said "Eat your eggs, Michel-angelo."

"I ain't hungry."

"I cooked these eggs because you assured me you were hungry," said Delilah.

Tom frowned at the eggs. Not good. Delilah had long ago reached her frowns-limit from her mother who was the very Mona Lisa of frowns.

"They're hard," said Tom, "I like 'em gooey."

Delilah shrugged, slammed his dish of eggs on the makeshift kitchen table, made two Nescafs, thrust the discarded flowery kimono at Tom, slammed one of the Nescafs before him, and motioned for him to sit, which he did, with an agonizing thump on the hardened cement sacks. Delilah leaned against the kitchen sink and still squinting with sleep sipped her coffee and ate her eggs.

"I'm real sorry I like them gooey," said her contrite cowboy, "I jist can't help it. Mom always made 'em that way"

"Then shove them up your arse, darling," said Delilah.

Tom was shocked. For a moment. Then drank some coffee, picked at his eggs and said plaintively, "Last night you said you loved me. You said it was love at first sight."

"Hell's ballocks! Did I?"

"Yeah." It was almost a whine. "Like five times. I counted."

An impossible situation was getting out of hand. Must be rectified -- and pronto. So, as earnestly as possible Delilah said: "Last night I was very lonely, very horny and sozzled. This morning I am not at all lonely, not at all horny, very tired, very hung-over, very sober, and a hundred years older than you are."

"I love you. You said you loved me too. You said it was love at first sight! Don't that mean anything to you?!"

"If there is anything I don't want, Gerald, it's a squalid little marriage!"

This was Delilah's years old, melodrama party-turn, her one and only, put to good use at last.

"Huh?! Who's Gerald?"

"You're intimating it, Gerald, with those impossibly blue eyes of yours!"

"Huh?!"

"Don't let's reach for the moon, Gerald, when we have the stars!"

"Who the heck is Gerald? Who the heck said anything about stars? Who the heck said anything about gettin' married? I'm too darn young, like, to get married."

"It was a joke, cowboy, only Canadian Snow Geese and cretins bother to marry anymore. Marriage is subjugation. If ever I were mad enough to contemplate another marriage it would be to a one hundred year old, terminally ill billionaire."

There was a great pause, and Delilah was certain Tom was about to cry. But he said softly "When I marry it will be to somebody exactly like you..."

Delilah was overcome and felt herself at the edge of the horrifying snort that always preceded her tears.

"...Only not so old," finished far-too-young Tom.

Delilah recovered instantly. Much relieved, though she couldn't put her finger on quite why, she exclaimed very slightly hysterically, "Listen!" and she whistled a few notes. "What's that?"

Tom shook his head.

"The Scarf Dance."

"Please, I..."

"Listen!" Delilah frantically whistled a few more notes. What's that?"

Tom shook his head. He was serious, and dammit, she wouldn't be.

"Rustles of Spring!" This completed her musical repertoire. "What's this?" She whistled again.

Tom, who seemed either about to cry or shout, sadly shook his head again.

It's the "Scarf Dance, goddamn it! I whistled it before! Don't you ever listen?"

"What's your name? Why won't you, like, tell me your name?"

"My name is Delilah."

"I love you, Delilah."

"Put on your trousers, cowboy."

Tom took Delilah's coffee from her, set it on kitchen sink, took her hands in his. "You were my first woman."

"Dee-li-lah. Dee-li-lah. Delilah." He said it again and again. "You're like, exotic, Delilah, jist like your name is. You're like, exotic."

"In name only. I'm known for cutting hair."

"Why? Are you a hairdresser, honey bun?"

She sighed and rolled over in bed to be that bit

farther away from him. She must learn to keep herself out of foolish mischief like this. She had warned herself, sure -- he was a child-man. But so attractive, so innocent. Was it her own, barely remembered, innocence that drew her to him in this worst possible way? Or was it pure lust? After a moment she settled again for pure lust. But whatever it was, it must be held at bay, be kept separate from her woman within. Or disaster would surely ensue.

"Are you a hairdresser?" repeated Tom, gently turning her face to his.

"No. I'm a chanteuse."

Tom was perplexed.

"I sing, kid." Where had the *kid* come from? Had this infant barbarian dredged up her American past? Was it coming back to haunt her, O.K. Corral guy and all?

Suddenly, Delilah sprang, singing, out of bed, began to dress. "Two different worlds, we live in two different worlds..."

Tom crawled out of the bedclothes, sat on the edge of the bed and spread his arms to Delilah.

"Kiss me, my singin' darlin'!"

"Get dressed, love. I'll show you London by night."

"We jist spent, like, the whole darn day in bed!" he said, pulling on his stars and stripes Y-fronts. "I never spent the whole darn day in bed in my whole darn life!"

"Another first, cowboy! Congratulations! First lay, first darn day!"

Tom, half-dressed, pulled her back to the bed. She didn't resist. "You men want one thing only! But what the hell!" and she flopped herself gracelessly into his arms.

The next morning, Nigel opened his back door. The little dog dashed out, ran directly to the potted lilac, cocked its leg and peed. This occurred at approximately the same time that Delilah, tired and clay-dusted from early work in her garage pottery, entered the bathroom to find Tom in the bathtub.

"Oh, there you are. Had a good lie-in? How's the hang-over?"

Delilah went to the wash basin, held out her hand to him. "Soap."

"Were those really men in that pub last night?" he said reaching the soap to her. She laughed, said "Yes, love, men dressed as women."

"Oh?" he said. "We have those in San Francisco too! I've heard about it!"

She soaped her face, said "Zat so? Takes yer breath away, don't it?!" and looked for the flannel. Tom had it. She held out her hand. "Flannel"

"Huh?"

"Wash cloth."

He handed it to her. "You're beautiful, Delilah."
Then that look again. That adoring puppy-dog look.

"You're all hyped up, son. You watch too much freaking television." She looked down her nose at him.

"You're a raving beauty, Delilah!"

"I do rave and though I am alarmingly charming I'm not, by any stretch of the imagination, beautiful."

"You are!"

"I'm only a comely working woman, and you, sir, are a lazy lout who lolls the day away in bed and bath whilst I labour for a loaf."

"I like your... words, Delilah. I like the words you use."

Delilah yanked a towel from a nail in the wall, patted her face dry. "Then you're easily impressed, young man." She was feeling older every minute and threw the towel at him.

Tom rose from the bath and began to dry himself.

"What you say always, like, means something."

Delilah began to scrub her nails with a brush. "Why shouldn't it? What would be the point of saying anything if it didn't actually mean something?"

"Did you mean what you said about marriage?"

"Not for me. I've tried it."

"Wasn't he, like, good to you?"

"We weren't good to each other."

"I'll bet it was his fault. Because you're, like, perfect."

"We were equally at fault. Let's talk about something else. Ouch," she said, catching a brush bristle under her nail.

"Is this too... like, painful for you?"

"No darling, too... like, boring for me."

"Shall I tell you about Hopwood Hollow?"

"Hopwood Hollow?!"

"My hometown."

In despair, Delilah examined her rough-skinned fingers and broken fingernails and sighed "Tell me about Hopwood Hollow."

Tom was pleased, dropped his towel on the floor, grabbed his newly-laundered-by-Delilah, shorts and pulled them on. "It's awful little, Hopwood Hollow. There's a river, well, almost a river, runnin' right down the middle." He slipped into his newly laundered t-shirt as Delilah retrieved his towel from the wet bathroom floor and dried her hands.

"Hopwood Hollow," repeated Delilah.

"I guess it sounds awful funny, don't it?" he said and stepped into his newly laundered by you-know-who jeans.

"Yeah," said Delilah, smiling. "I guess it does.

What's a hollow?"

"A hunk gouged out of a hill, like, I guess."

"By glacial action?"

"By what?"

"A big glacier carved it out of the hill during the last great Ice Age."

"Oh! Do ya think so?! Wowwwww!" Tom smiled lovingly at her. "You're like, different, darling."

This stopped Delilah for a moment but she recovered and said "So are you, cowboy. Pull on your boots. You're going to help me today."

After stopping three times to requisition several abandoned bricks at various deserted building sites -- Delilah did not intend to waste Tom's two muscular arms -- they arrived at a builder's market where he loaded a small sack of cement into the boot of the Midget. A young woman behind the cash window handed Delilah her change and receipt and whistled. "Your son's a dish! Where'd he get his hot cowboy kit?!"

"Hopwood Hollow!" Delilah said sharply.

"I only asked," said the young woman who quickly recovered and wrote something on a scrap of paper. "My telephone number, Missus. Give this to your son, please."

Tom, at the car, looked up, smiled at both of them

but particularly at the young woman. This was noted by Delilah as she tore the young woman's scrap of paper into tiny bits she discarded behind her and returned to instruct Tom about the proper arrangement of a cement sack that did not interfere with the crucial closing of ones car boot.

When they returned to the mews Tom attempted to remove the problematic cement sack. Nigel, exercising his dog on a leash for a change, suddenly appeared at the near end of the mews and ambled toward them. "Exploitin' the labour of children, are we?" called her hairy-bellied next door neighbour whom Delilah haughtily ignored. Chuckling, Nigel unleashed the dog and followed it down the mews, revelling in the antics of the loathsome creature as it dashed to and fro pissing on everything in its path.

Joanna's window opened and she looked out, sized up the labouring Tom who had not yet been able to extract the cement sack from the Midget's boot.

"Good morning all!" she cried.

"Morning, Jo," called Delilah, who laboured with Tom knowing that she alone could have done it all in half the time with half the trouble. "Half the trouble!" she muttered and despaired, adding "Who am I? What am I? Where the fuck did I come from? Where am I going?" At the moment even her woman within was without a clue.

"Brick wall time?" called Joanna from her window.

"A small beginning," puffed Delilah from one end of the stubborn cement sack.

"Certainly is, you old cradle-snatcher!" teased Joanna, "a very small beginning!"

Delilah left the cement to Tom, approached Joanna and whispered. "I assure you, Jo. There is nothing small about him." Delilah enjoyed bragging about her young conquest. In the same way she knew he would brag, no doubt chopping at least ten years off her age, when he returned to God's country and was among his colleagues -- no that wasn't quite the right word. His bro's? His dudes?

"He's beautiful!" said Joanna.

"Keep it down, love. Your Darren might hear you and Daddy might spank."

"Darren's sleeping."

"Thought he might be." Delilah checked her wristwatch. "It's only three-thirty."

"We had a busy night! I am happy to report that we're coping! We coped all night!"

"So did we!"

"With a nod at Tom, Joanna whispered, "A bit young, isn't he?"

"Not that young," replied Delilah, more irritated

with herself than with Joanna.

"He is that young, Delilah."

"Tom!" yelled Delilah.

"Yeah?!" said Tom, who was still labouring with the cement sack which was now tightly lodged between several purloined bricks and an ancient scythe.

"Tom, how old are you?!"

"Seventeen!"

"He's eighteen if he's a day," said Delilah. "He literally fell on me at John Lewis, you jealous cow."

"Me, jealous? Not at all, love, I prefer grown men who build things."

Delilah, who now decided that Tom could not manage alone, said "Bye, bye, Jo."

Joanna waved, smiled, took a long, appraising look at Tom and shut her window.

"Having trouble, love? Can't cope?" said Delilah.

Tom nodded helplessly. Delilah climbed onto the boot, planted her feet firmly and with one mighty heave, dislodged the cement sack from its complex tangle of bricks, and the scythe, a cherished gift from a recently deceased elderly mews neighbour whose charming sweet shop at the end of the mews was even now being transformed as a pied-à-terre for some posh stiff.

Delilah skipped out of the boot, grunted, swung

the small but heavy cement sack over her shoulder and marched to her decrepit, little house. "Be a love, darling, and open the gate."

Tom was immersed in an erotic medley of awe and admiration for this glamorous older woman who knew just what she wanted. But he obeyed forthwith and opened the gate to the little garden between hers and Nigel's houses.

Delilah dropped the cement sack just beside her potted lilac and grinned happily at Tom. "There'll be a brick wall here one day, love. His freaking dog pees on my potted lilac and will not, cannot, be tolerated. Did you see him leer at me?"

"The dog?" asked Tom.

"No. Nigel. The yobbo next door. Are you being clever?"

"Huh?"

"I take that back," she said quickly. "Nigel is a filthy, pot-bellied, string-vested yobbo. Men like that don't even like women. They want one thing only from a woman."

Tom put an arm around Delilah's waist, nudged closer. "Errr, shall we?"

"And that's it! Let's get those bricks out of the car first, then, yes, please."

"Do you believe in fate?" asked Tom, balancing his tea on his bare stomach as they lay happily exhausted in bed.

"How d'you mean, love?"

"That it is our...like, our...like..."

"Destiny?" coached Delilah.

"Yeah. Our destiny," said Tom as, to Delilah's chagrin, the early afternoon sun lighted his extraordinary angel's face. "Like in horoscopes -- our destiny to, like, love... each other."

Delilah scowled slightly, in a way she hoped was engaging, not off-putting, but enough to change the subject. "Turn off your telly, love. You are a naive darling." She hugged him. "But very nice for a foreigner."

"Your real honest, Delilah. Your a real straight-shooter."

Delilah studied Tom for a moment, decided she was pleased.

"Who's Jimmy? That sign over your garage?" he asked.

"Jimmy's Auto Repair. It was there when I came. I left it. Discourages rapists."

"It didn't discourage you," said Tom, "You're, like, real lonely, ain't you?"

Delilah, taken by surprise said quickly, "Isn't everybody? Sometimes? Jee-sus, I sound like a character in a cheap romantic novel."

"What was your husband like?" asked Tom.

"Here I go again, Barbara Cartland," she muttered under her breath. "He was all right. We were all wrong."

"You and me are all right," said Tom, more fervently than was appreciated.

Delilah felt herself stumbling once more into dangerous territory. "Better than average," she whispered, trembling the tiniest bit.

"What luck!" said Tom and hugged her so hard she nearly choked.

"It was my lucky shilling," she said and decided on the spot that this conversation was going much too far for comfort. So she climbed out of bed, threw on a robe, went to the window and bent out and could just see, on the ledge over her ground floor front window, Phyllis's shining shilling. Tom joined her and she pointed to it. "Have you got ten P, love?"

"Wow," said Tom, "I'm a little, like, short."

Delilah grabbed ten P from her jacket, tangled in the bedclothes. Whispering to herself, she reached out the window and placed the coin as near as she could reach beside the shilling. "Lucky us."

"Poor Phyllis, poor dear. There she was, drunk as they come, up to her hips in the top of my car. She'd climbed onto it to reach her lucky shilling and fallen through. She and Jimmy had put it there years ago when my garage pottery was his car repair."

"A true love story. Like us, like," said Tom wiping a tear from a glistening, impossibly blue eye. Tom wasn't supposed to be so...so freaking sensitive. This instigated Delilah's traditional, pathetic snort which lapsed instantly, and as always, into a flood of tears. "Stop that! She blubbed, I can't bear bawl-babies!"

Tom hugged her close. They lay, eyes streaming as the real world stopped for her and seemed, at least seemed, to stop for him as well. It was replaced by an improbable dream of bliss and romantic rubbish that for some reason began very, so very slowly to become rancid, began to smell a lot like servitude. Like ten wasted years. Delilah needed to salvage what was left of her and this was quite enough fairy tale for two days. School was out, kiddies! Still.

"For the Chunnel train, cowboy. You'll be hungry."

Tom was packing his backpack as Delilah finished making a sandwich, wrapped it carefully, dropped it on a small pile of similarly wrapped sandwiches, put the pile in a paper bag and the bag in Tom's hand.

"Gee thanks!" said Tom, "jist like Mom's!"

"Gee...like, thanks," said Delilah.

Tom laid the sandwiches in his backpack, said "I hear France is great, like!"

"Oh yes, great in the definitive sense," said Delilah. "Louis XIV, Napoleon..."

"Nap who? Who's that?"

Delilah was wordless. She attempted to imagine the almost touching ignorance from whence Tom's remark sprang. Helpless, she shrugged. No. Tom was not a sensation with words. Or history or... But still? No. No *still* could be appropriate here, whispered Delilah's woman within.

Near the station, after stopping to snatch up four stray bricks from a building site, they were fortunate to screech into, as the previous occupant moved out of, the only parking space for miles.

"Don't forget, I'm comin' back!" said Tom, beaming lovingly into Delilah's eyes.

"I won't hold my breath," said Delilah kindly, even rather sadly.

"Huh?" said Tom.

"Nothing, cowboy."

"I'll, like, miss you."

"I'll, like, miss you, too, Tom," she said, wondering if she would but hoping she wouldn't.

"I'll always love you, Delilah. You were my first woman."

This really was going too far! "Were?!" exclaimed Delilah.

But there was time for no more. "Hey!" yelled Tom at the top of his voice. "Hey, Debbie! Hey, Debbie!" he yelled and leapt out of the Midget leaving Delilah wordless again. He was suddenly hugging a fearfully attractive young woman attached to another American-flagged backpack.

"Debbie, baby! Where have you been?! I been lookin' all over London! You were supposed to be at McDonald's yesterday!"

"I *was* at McDonald's yesterday!" she cried with a scorching glance at Delilah. "Where were you, Tommy?!"

"I was there, honey bun!"

"Like hell you were!" hissed Delilah under her breath.

Debbie stuck out her lower lip in a pout. "I didn't see you, Tommy. I waited like, two hours!"

Delilah sat gaping in her miserable little Midget, at 'Tommy' who was thinking fast. "McDonald's on Piccadilly like we planned, baby?" he said.

"No! McDonald's on Haymarket! Oh, Tommy!" cried Debbie.

Tom hugged her and Debbie literally melted.

How does she do that?! thought Delilah, still gaping. Was this some freaking CGI effect?! Am I in some Sci-Fi alternate universe?! How the fuck could a woman actually melt into that over-muscled idiot-child's arms after his obvious lie?! Has she no freaking respect, like, for herself? Has she no intuition? Has she no unique *anything* within?!

Debbie hugged 'Tommy' lovingly, as Delilah sat speechless, vibrating with rage, in her half-roofed, feeble excuse for a car -- Mum was freaking correct! -- as 'Tommy' shot a quick, worried glance in her direction.

"Oh Tommy," cried Debbie, "I thought I had, like, lost you I was so miserable! Oh, Tommy! I was so sad. And now I am so glad!"

"The girl is a trained logician!" muttered Delilah.

"If you hadn't of, like, been here today I don't know what I would of done!" Then suddenly: "Who's she?!"

Delilah simply couldn't believe it as this simpering excuse for a sentient female actually pointed an accusing finger directly at her!

Tom backed the tiniest bit away from Debbie. "Oh, *her*," he said, smoothly gesturing toward Delilah.

"Yeah," muttered Delilah from her Midget, "*her*."

"I hitched a ride, like, to the train station."

Debbie cast a suspicious look at Delilah, said, "A ride, like, to the train station?"

"Yeah. A ride, like, to the train station," said Tom and gulped.

"Yeah. But let's just call it a ride, kiddies," muttered Delilah, grim and dangerous as the balding tires on her Midget.

"You look tired, Tommy," mewed a deeply concerned Debbie.

"Yeah. I haven't had much sleep. Europe sure is noisy," groaned Tom.

"Yeah," I think so too," groaned Debbie.

"Yeah, isn't it? We never, like, seem to get used to it," groaned Delilah and rolled her eyes, and sprang out and opened the car boot where she waited, her spine tingling unpleasantly.

"You better get your stuff, baby, from that woman," said Debbie, making it clear that his stuff was now her stuff. "We'll be late for our Chunnel train."

"Oh. Yeah," answered Tom who hesitantly inched towards Delilah, nodded sheepishly, and began to remove his backpack from the boot.

"Need, like, help, baby?" said Delilah, fawning furiously.

"Errr...no thanks, Miss."

"Hurry, Tommy! We'll be late!" said Debbie, with an ugly look at Delilah who with a haughty smile ostentatiously ignored her.

"Yeah, Tommy, hurry, honey, you'll be late, like!" called Delilah, her voice thundering over the busy street.

"Thanks," said Tom "for...errr..."

"For, like, everything?" said Delilah.

"Errrrrrr, Yeah," managed Tom.

"Think nothing of it, darling. I don't," said Delilah. "And I wouldn't eat those sandwiches I made for you," she whispered, "I believe the mayonnaise has gone right off. Brunch on the Chunnel train is called for, Tommy. Maybe Mom has pinned your lunch money in your pocket?"

"Err, yeah. Well, err, so long. See ya."

"Not if I see you first."

"Huh?"

Debbie stamped her foot. "Tommm-mmmmy, we'll be late!"

Tom hoisted on his backpack and Delilah angrily banged shut the boot lid. Tom waved perfunctorily at her as she screeched away in the Midget giving him a vivid two-finger stuff-you.

"What did that mean? The sign that old woman made from her rusty old car?"

"V for victory, I guess, like what old Winston Churchill used to do."

"Who's that?"

"Some old king," said Tom, looking sadly over his shoulder at the speedily departing Delilah as he and Debbie, backpacked and American flagged, disappeared into the railway station.

Delilah sped along, not so carefully as she ought, her mouth, like Mum's, set in a mean red line, her eyes glinting as she ran Tom's voice over and over in her head.

"Delilah. You were my first woman," said Tom, the liar.

Delilah shifted gears and yelled "My arse!" to the wind whipping through her wretched little car's rotten canvas top. She slammed on her brakes at a red light, skidded to a stop.

"Your real honest, Delilah."

"Ha!" she shouted, "Unlike certain people I know!"

The light went green and the suitably enraged Delilah in her maligned Midget careened down a nearly empty side street.

In the mews at last, she skidded to a stop, rocketed from her car and careened into her hovel of a house. Through exposed beamed walls and wacko unfinished plumbing and tangled electric wires she flew. Up the ladder-like stairs and into the bedroom she hurtled. There, she slammed open the window, leaned dangerously far out, ripped her pullover on a nail, cursed violently, and snatched back the ten P coin she and Tom had placed on the ledge by Phyllis's special shilling. She pulled herself back through the window and was angrily rubbing the scratched elbow in her torn pullover when she spotted the illegally unleashed rat-dog as it came sniffing, urinating and pooping down the mews. Disgusted, she watched the rodent-like creature for a moment then, when it was close enough for her to see the whites of its eyes, she leaned out the window and hurled the ten P coin at the odious animal with such force and precision that, struck squarely on its nose, the dog emitted a yelp so dreadful that Nigel's door, as well as several windows in the mews, were flung open in terror. Delilah whisked her curtains shut before Nigel could see her. He peered suspiciously up and down the mews as the dog cowered between his ankles and crept, whimpering, into the house.

Nigel scratched the exposed belly beneath his string vest, took a last, vain look up and down the mews and closed the door. Delilah watched it all through a crack in her curtains and dropped herself on her recently-occupied-by-two, bed, pre-snorted, sobbed for a moment. Then began to laugh.

As Delilah laughed, and it would be a long laugh, Nigel inched open his back door and rat-dog shot out, made a beeline directly to Delilah's lilac, sniffed it, cocked a leg, reconsidered, deserted the lilac, trotted to her glass kitchen door, sniffed, cocked a leg and was about to pee but spotted the cement sack Delilah and Tom had earlier left beside the potted lilac and pissed on it instead. Then, as a seeming afterthought, if animals are allowed to entertain such, returned to the kitchen door and pissed on that too.

3

DELILAH HARASSES
MIDDLE-MANAGEMENT

Mum always slept soundly in Delilah's surprisingly comfortable bed. This was because during Mum's overnights Delilah was forced to sleep on the uncomfortable, chesterfield sofa in that rubbish tip her only child foolishly called a living room. Her daughter's acute discomfort, reasoned Mum, would drive Delilah to a speedier completion of this mad, mews project that was ruining Mum's life. And fortunately, Delilah's as well.

From the kitchen downstairs the clatters of breakfast climaxed in a dropped frying pan's reverberating crash. Mum woke suddenly, sat up and attempted to get her bearings. It was a given, getting ones bearings in this makeshift chaos that was the condom-strung, centre ring of Delilah's new single-life's circus tent.

Mum slipped silently from her daughter's bed and began a quick snoop of the bedroom before breakfast would arrive. She sifted through a stack of cardboard boxes filled with linens and towels and pullovers, and sourly noted the large hole in the elbow of a once expensive, cashmere pullover. Elbow holes were a common failing of her impossible daughter.

Mum winced at the unspeakable disorder of this bare-boards-unfinished bedroom. Then, her eyes narrowing to slits, she crept back to the bedside table, pulled out a drawer and ejected a tiny, yet intense, squeak as she spied the notorious plump envelope! Mum had expressly removed those condoms from the premises yet Delilah had sneaked them back! Mum's mouth set in that familiar thin, red line. She snatched up the plump envelope as though it were hot coals and crammed it into her coat pocket just as Delilah entered with a tray of tea and toast for her and a coffee for herself.

"Here you are, Mumsy."

"Do not call me Mumsy, makes me sound old."

"You are old, darling."

"Old-er, not old. I am not as old as you are, Delilah, for your age."

Delilah, already chewing on her own bit of toast, said "Food for thought."

"Don't talk with your mouth full, dear," cautioned Mum as Delilah placed the breakfast tray before her and sat opposite with her coffee.

"It would be so much easier, darling, if you could come downstairs for breakfast," said Delilah reasonably.

"And set foot in that pigsty of a kitchen? No thank you very much." Mum nibbled daintily at her toast, eager to continue this decorous example for her daughter. But Delilah remained secretly revolted by the endless, tiny bites and chews Mum thought necessary to dismantle a simple bit of crisp toast in her mouth.

"I suppose I needn't comment, Delilah, on the shocking state of your bedroom."

"Right you are, Mumsy. As you already have, you needn't."

"But I shall," insisted her mother, "If Joyce Grudden ever saw this room, yours truly's name would be yours truly mud."

"Put your troubled mind at ease, darling. Joyce Grudden will never see this room."

"She might. Miss Grudden has her ways." Mum nibbled, sipped, then frowned violently. "She saw your Trevor yesterday in the company of a pleasant woman. A pleasant woman! Your Trevor was..."

"He is not my Trevor, Mum. Not anymore." These words remained an indelible loop inside Delilah's head, destined to be repeated now and, it seemed, forever.

Mum sat up stiffly, yanked another pillow behind her back and continued in a voice of harrowing authority. "You were married to your Trevor for ten years, my girl! Your Trevor can safely be referred to as yours. At least in my lingo!"

"How's the tea, dear?"

"This pleasant woman of Trevor's is thought by Joyce Grudden to already reside with Trevor who is now teetering on the precipice of re-situating himself," said Mum, evening class poetry rampant.

"Re-situating, ha! And I know exactly where," said Delilah. "How's your tea, Mumsy dear?"

"Awful. Alas. I blame myself. I never taught you to make a proper cuppa."

Mum took another miniscule bite of toast and Delilah shuddered. "It's an art," declared Mum, "that I surrendered. To my cost, I gave up. You would never listen. Never." Mum sipped again, daintily, girlishly, delicately as she could under such cruel circumstances. "Mea culpa. Mea maxima culpa!" wailed wide-eyed miserable Mum and swatted at what might have been a tear, but wasn't.

"Your poetry class, darling? How goes the poetry night out? Dramatically satisfying?"

"I am told by our instructor that, for my age, I am a phenomenon."

"Long known to me, my sweet. But, as such, you must also know that making a cup of tea is a man's job. Or should be."

"Such ideas will not take you far in life." Mum gestured petulantly at the unfinished bedroom with her piece of toast. "Indeed, haven't. This bedroom, Delilah, is mute testimony to that. Mute testimony."

"How often do you attend this poetry class of yours?" asked Delilah.

"Twice a week."

"Perhaps you might cut back to once a week, darling. Your lyrical phrases threaten to engulf us," said Delilah, grinning. Mum was not to be sidetracked, and now thrust her toast directly at Delilah. "You can't even make a proper bit of toast."

"It's good, healthy wholemeal!" parried Delilah.

"The substance is immaterial! It's how you prepare it that counts. Alas, I am mea culpa there too."

"What about this pleasant woman Trevor was seen with?" said Delilah, from behind the a gulp of coffee.

Mum ignored Delilah's rude gurgle and replied "Ah! We're interested, are we?"

"I'll bite," said her only daughter. "Who is she?"

"Joyce isn't quite sure yet. We're working on it. This pleasant woman knows how to dress. Which is more..."

"...than I can say for you, Delilah," said Delilah.

"You said it, my girl, not me."

"I stick to a budget, Mummy dear, I can't afford designer labels any more. Nor would I buy them if I could. With a little imagination in arranging a proper ensemble, Marks and Spencer is good enough for me."

"Marks and Spencer's are not one of your label couturiers, are they? Joyce Grudden wouldn't be caught dead in a Marks and Spencer's label."

"If I remember rightly, It would take more than a label to cover the Grudden arse," said Delilah with a girlish giggle that very nearly amused her mother.

"Language!" said Mum with the merest shadow of a smile. "Joyce Grudden gravitates towards your finer, upward mobile, high street couturiers."

"Such as?"

"You'd have to ask Joyce," said Mum snootily.

"Since I do not intend to ask Ms Grudden the time of day I suggest we drop the subject. I'm a raga-muffin, Mum. I was born a ragamuffin and I shall die a ragamuffin."

"Rubbish! Ragamuffins are made not born. You've simply become understandably selfish and sluttish since you've not been comfortable in marriage. Hardship has coarsened you. Forewarned is forearmed, my girl. You had better strike fast before Trevor gets himself situated and too comfortable with..."

"...his pleasant woman," said Delilah.

"She is well-dressed, half your age and wears designer labels from her head to her well-heeled, heels! So my advice to you, daughter, is to get comfortable in designer labels and the highest heels you can salvage at your local thrift shop. Just butt right in and give this pleasant woman the old heave-ho! That over-dressed hussy! That home-breaker!"

"Darling! There is no home to break!" cried Delilah.

"There will be, If you'll do just as I say! Strike now! Whilst the iron is hot! Go back to Trevor for just a while, dear. Make him buy you a whole wardrobe of expensive things then take off! Be sensible. If you don't want Trevor you've still got to find someone. Wake up, Delilah! Cast your jeans into the fires of hell! You'll need a proper ensemble for the hunt!"

Delilah solemnly took both of Mum's hands in hers, smiled patiently. "My dear, there will be no ex-husband hunt. Or any husband hunt. Another marriage is not on my agenda. I have no intention of ever going back to Trevor or of him coming back to me. It is over, darling. Over."

"Woe is me!" said Mum and snatched her hands away from Delilah, took up a piece of toast and, with many tiny, staccato nibbles, finally absorbed it.

"There are a few things of mine I'd like to get back," said Delilah. "A few things in a trunk in Trevor's attic. Clothes."

"Clothes?" replied Mum suspiciously.

"My fake monkey fur, in particular. It's my favourite fake fur."

"Not that horror again, Delilah! You wore it to a Halloween party when you were seventeen! You looked like a child-prostitute! I'm surprised you weren't impounded."

"I fancy it," said Delilah dipping poignantly into her days of wild abandon before the real world so savagely sunk in. "It's in style again."

"If you're a tart. All your tarts, prossies and vagrants wear them," said Mum.

"If that pleasant woman is living with Trevor and if she is as pleasant as Ms Grudden asserts, perhaps she will let me come in to fetch my fake monkey fur. Trevor has offered it back but I don't wish to see him on our old territory. He gloats."

"He does not gloat. Your Trevor is a gentleman

through and through."

"Of course he is, dear. In his way. Just not my gentleman," said Delilah, determined not to demolish Mum's agreeable fantasies the way Trevor had demolished hers a week after their wedding. "Drink your tea, Mumsy, or we'll miss your train."

'Mumsy' glowered at Delilah, drank the last of her tea. Delilah took up the breakfast tray and went downstairs. Mum rose, dressed quickly, and felt a tiny surge of pleasure as she pictured the plump envelope safely concealed in her hugely-flapped coat pocket under a seldom used, silk emergency scarf. Smiling wickedly into a large piece of cracked mirror Delilah had taped on the wall, she applied her lipstick. Mum felt that she was quite fetching for her age and, whatever their quarrels, her daughter would agree. This happy thought encouraged an easier continuation to an otherwise grim morning.

After Mum had been installed on her train Delilah took several curly-tailed pigs and two smiling frogs from their moulds and set them out to dry on a shelf with many, too many, others. They were her most popular line. But even they were not selling well enough to keep her pottery business out of the red. Plastics were taking over. This did not bode well for the future of ceramics. She was in the wrong flaming business and she knew freaking zilch about Plastics except that she'd recently heard a rumour, couldn't remember where, that even Funfair Kewpies were now made of plastic. In China. Or was it Thailand?

At her desk, early that evening, a cup of tea, and pen and ink beside her, Delilah sat down to write an important letter that also had been much on her mind. Despite Joanna's urgings Delilah had resisted sticking even a token toe back into the cyber-world she had deserted since her divorce. The Internet was still under consideration. But only, Delilah was cautioned by her woman within, only as a last resort.

Just now Delilah had to attractively clothe her one-year-old divorcee's frame. So she, with flourishes grand, wrote her letter with a real pen and real ink. Would that it were a feathered quill. But that would be going too far. She was more modern than mad.

Dear Someone at Marks and Spencer:
I am a loyal though occasionally dowdy customer of yours -- dowdy in attire only. As my shape and posture are a knockout. Sadly, I found myself defending you to my mother today. Mum thinks your clothes, for a woman like me (at the ripe old age of thirty-two years last month), lack inspiration and so, sadly, upon reflection, do I. I have a reasonably full bust, a modestly

small waist and am somewhat shorter than average but not what you'd call petite. Perhaps "comely" would be more accurate. I have recently had increasing difficulty dressing myself from the racks of Marks and Spencer and thought, were I in your place, I should certainly wish to know why.

What I require is simplicity: Blouses without bows, jackets without piping, shoes without tassels, underwear, please, without flowery patterns. And the cut -- please, some space. I am not busty but I do have adequate cleavage to contain without appearing like a burst sausage. I would be pleased to show you my body if it would help. I am sure there are millions like me out here.

In closing let me say that it is us ample but normal sized people who have made you what you are today, successful, and for the most part, responsive to our comments. Hence my letter.

Yours sincerely, An occasionally dowdy (but not by choice) customer.

Ms. Delilah Davies.

PS: Enclosed is a recent photo with telephone number on back.

Two weeks later Delilah received an answer:

Dear Ms. Davies:
From your enclosed photo it is apparent you
are far from dowdy, apparel notwithstanding. The fault, if there is one, must surely be
ours. In closing, might I suggest we meet for
a drink and talk? We are always interested
in the informed opinions of our customers.
I shall, if I may, ring you at the number you
have so considerately provided.
Yours with thanks, very sincerely,
        Andrew Atkins,
Customer relations representative,
Marks and Spencer.
PS: Be assured, Ms Davies, that your age, of
thirty-two, is hardly what we at Marks and
Spencer would call "ripe old"

Delilah read Andrew Atkins' letter to a morose
but trying-to-be-interested Joanna who, a cup of tea
in hand, reclined on the junk-stacked sofa. "Andrew
Atkins and Delilah Davies. You sound like a couple
of movie stars. I hope you hit it off, love. It's tough
coping on your lonesome. I know. Incidentally, I
thought you were thirty-nine."

"I fudged a bit, love."

"Understandably!" said Joanna.

Delilah gave Joanna a dark look but continued amicably. "This 'Atkins' sounds stuffy. I don't think I'll like him. No. Certain I won't. He probably dictated this letter and some underpaid woman had to type it."

"At least she's got a job!"

It took a second for this to penetrate. "Oh, Jo! No!"

"Yes. As of today's post. I let you read your letter first." Joanna slapped her own letter into Delilah's hand.

"Oh, Jo!" exclaimed Delilah, "This is awful! They can't do this to you!"

"Can and did!" wailed Joanna, "It's no surprise. She would and I wouldn't."

"Who would?"

"Janet Simpson would," sniffled Joanna.

"Janet Simpson would what?"

"Janet Simpson would fetch coffee for the reptile like you said I shouldn't! So I didn't! As I wouldn't!"

The tears began.

"Correct!" said Delilah, "you shouldn't, wouldn't, and didn't! You're an executive assistant, not a dog's body!" Then it came to her suddenly, "Hell's ballocks! I am indirectly responsible!"

Through her tears, Joanna said distinctly "Directly responsible, more like. I wouldn't have had the nerve to do it on my own!"

"Now stop that, love! You know I can't bear blubberers!"

Delilah successfully fought back her own presob snort. After a moment Joanna quietened down and said "In a way, you're right, Delilah. But I'd rather have a job than be right all the time like you are."

"Jo, I am sincerely sorry about this but it is for the best. You should rejoice. No more looking into those beady reptilian eyes. No more pinches on your arse."

"He never pinched me, Delilah. Not anywhere!" said Joanna fighting back more tears.

"That's as may be but we shall take this to the highest authorities as a test case! Meanwhile..."

"Meanwhile what?" sobbed Joanna.

"Meanwhile, your Darren can pay rent and stop living off you!"

"But he can't Delilah! He's skint! Broke! He's a student again! Remember?!"

"This happened rather suddenly, didn't it?"

"We decided," Joanna went on.

"Who decided?"

"Well," Joanna continued, tearfully blowing her nose, "Darren said now that he was living with me he could afford to quit his job and go back to school and be better qualified and make bags of money for us both. But now I've lost my job we don't even have enough to buy food for Mikie! I don't know how we'll cope!"

"At least you don't have rent to pay," said Delilah triumphantly. "Your father gave you your house here, free and clear, didn't he? When you were living across the street from Trevor and me? Hey! What about asking your father for money?"

"Daddy's dead, Delilah! He's dead! Don't you ever listen?!"

"God, Jo! I'm so sorry! When's the funeral?"

"Five years ago!"

"Oh, dear! You can work for me in the pottery," said Delilah, eager as always to extend her calloused, helping hand. Especially as she was chief shit-stirrer of this whole anti-management soup.

"You don't have enough work as it is," said Joanna, wiping her eyes on a torn paper towel she found embedded behind the sofa cushion. "Garden goddesses are not popular just now. It isn't easy for you either."

"Not to fear, dear old friend. We can mould those little novelty kewpie dolls they give away as funfair prizes!"

"Oh, Delilah," moaned Joanna, "They make them of plastic now. In Thailand."

"Ballocks! That's where I heard it! Then we'll move kewpies up-market! We could make thousands.

It'd be easy. I can make two high quality kewpies for every pig -- a kewpie would be much faster, no curly tails to mould, less breakage. They would even be easier than the smiling frogs with their freaking painted eyelashes. You could do the book-work and marketing research!"

"Delilah, do you really think it will work?"

"No. Go on the dole, Joanna. We'll set up a sexual harassment suit against the reptile and sue the bastard to his company's knees, won't we?!"

"Yes! Oh yes! Yes! Yes!" cried Joanna, grasping at this last straw which she knew in her heart was offered by a loyal and sympathetic old friend who would do anything in the wide world to help. But who had no idea what in the wide world would.

Delilah rang the bell of a pleasant Georgian terraced house, her old home, on the Fulham edge of Chelsea. Mandy, red-eyed, opened the door. Delilah gasped and stared at her own some-years-ago self: Here was a striking, tarty-type in a tight, up-market T-shirt with "FRAGILE, HANDLE WITH CARE" emblazoned across her bust in silver sequins.

"Yeah?" said Mandy.

"Is Trevor in?"

"No. He's out."

"Good. Look, I'm his ex-wife. May I come in?"

"Why not?" replied Mandy, scratching at what Delilah knew was an irritating silver sequin just below a sumptuous breast. Delilah, at seventeen had worn a similarly sequinned T-shirt under her fake monkey fur at that Halloween Rave so many -- well not so many -- years before. Wait! This was it! The very same T-shirt! It was in her trunk beside the fake monkey fur and it was murder! The sequins went right through the cloth to what seemed like fish hooks inside which anchored them. Nobody, including herself, was allowed to touch her inflamed nipples for what seemed a millennium. Mandy's breasty message was indeed germane.

"May I ask if Trevor was expectin' you?" asked Mandy, scratching at another sequin and wiping away a tear.

"He was and he wasn't expecting me," said Delilah and entered her old home with a shudder.

"Take the weight off," said Mandy and directed her to a pricey, cretonne sofa that Delilah painfully recognized. Delilah walked wonderingly across the very large and essentially unchanged living room in the house that had not served her wisely or well for at least half of her ten year marriage to Trevor.

Wiping her eyes again, Mandy said "What d'you want then?"

"You have been crying. This is not a good sign,"

said Delilah, and sat, admitting to herself that there were far too many tears about recently and they seemed all to be coming from, herself included, women in varying degrees of complete disillusionment. She must speak to her woman within about this. When she had the time -- her unique woman, not her.

"It's nothin'," said Mandy, "What d'you want then?"

"Has Trevor left you?"

"Not a chance!" exclaimed Mandy with such virulent assurance that Delilah was flattened where she sat.

"What d'you want then?" asked Mandy yet again with precisely the same expression. This 'pleasant woman' was not happy, reasoned Delilah and shivered. God! How Trevor lurked in the very walls and grimy cracks between the floorboards -- especially in the grimy cracks between the floorboards in multiple rooms where his almost laughably unspeakable, adulterous deeds had been serially perpetrated!

"Trevor has abused you, hasn't he?!" said Delilah, several decibels louder than she'd meant.

"I said it's nothin!" protested Mandy, at the same volume. "What d'you want then, Miss ex-wife?" Her eyes were redder still.

"My fake monkey fur."

"That tatty old thing! I wore it twice. But no more. It makes my arse itch."

So that's it, thought Delilah incorrectly, tits and arse troubles, and stuck out her hand. "Glad to meet you, my name's Delilah."

"I know. I'm Mandy. Trevor told me all about you."

They shook hands and Delilah found herself saying, "I hope it was all good," and blushed. Mandy only gave her a dead-eyed assenting stare.

"I wouldn't wear that tatty old rag of a fur, darlin', it pongs."

"They all do," said Delilah.

"I wouldn't wear 'em then," replied Mandy.

"I'd kill for a cup of tea," said Delilah.

"Tea's off, love, but you're welcome to the kitchen. Everything's just where you left it. And then some."

Delilah rose and on her way to the kitchen said "If you don't do tea then who does? Trevor wouldn't go near the kitchen."

Mandy followed after Delilah. "We don't do tea. As a rule we eat out."

Delilah knew precisely where everything was. She filled the electric kettle, set a tea tray with cups and saucers she found in their familiar places, and year-old cookies from the freezer. She knew they were at least a year old because she had bought them. But she dropped them on the tray anyway. Though she had no intention of eating them herself and would warn Mandy away if she tried, they were yellow and pink-iced and decorative. God knows, this house of gloom longed for a treat. And how could such pretty little pastries really be poisonous?

"We always eat out," said Mandy. "I'm crackers for Chinese. Trevor's a spaghetti man. But then you'd know that, wouldn't you?"

"I am desperately afraid I would," said Delilah. "Why were you crying, love? What has Trevor done to you?"

"I'm not the domestic type." Ah. She was finally opening up. Alas, thought Delilah, the anguish men call forth in women! So, Mandy must be cheered up.

"You seem pleasant enough to me." Delilah clapped her hands, grinned ear to ear, "Make Trevor do the housework."

"Not a chance. We have a daily. Well. A twice-weekly but she won't iron, you see. I cry over ironing. It kills my immortal soul, know what I mean?"

"I think I do," said Delilah comfortingly.

"I'm not meant to drudge," said Mandy. "It's his shirts, see? Know what I mean?"

Delilah nodded the nod of a seasoned ironing-hater as she spotted a pile of shirts on her old ironing board.

"Trevor's bleedin' shirts make me cry." Mandy's eyes reddened again and it looked for a moment that she would. But she didn't, only made a 'fuck-you' sign at the ironing board.

Delilah, with a dark, unnerving frown Mum would have admired, said "Wait till you start finding lipstick on them."

"I have! I'm going bonkers! I have found lipstick on his bleedin' collar and it wasn't mine! Today!"

"Leave him. I did."

"I think I will!" cried Mandy. "The cheatin' bastard!"

"Can I drop you anywhere?" said Delilah, helpfully.

"Yes, thanks! At my Mum's please," replied Mandy.

"Just let me finish my cuppa, and we'll get my fake monkey fur and be off."

"Lovely! said Mandy, "I'll pack."

Mandy, dilemma free and happy at last, ran upstairs. The kettle whistled and Delilah prepared a pot. "Tea, Mandy?" she shouted up the staircase. "Tea and cookies?"

"What are 'cookies'?" called Mandy.

"Biscuits," called Delilah, "Biscuits with pretty icing on!"

"Oh yes, please!" cried Mandy from above, "Yes,

please! I'm dyin' for some nice biscuits and a good cuppa!"

Delilah was certain the cookies must be edible. She'd like some too. After all, she'd bought them. And they looked delicious!

Delilah was pleased with her day's work. When she got home she filled seven curly-tailed pig moulds and four smiling frogs. It had been a good day. She had earned, as Mum used to say, her cocoa. And tonight she was to meet Andrew Atkins of Marks and Sparks. She hoped he wasn't too stuffy.

Elegantly swathed in her fake monkey fur, Delilah hunched grimly over an empty table near this up-market, pub's entrance. She waited impatiently, her eyes on the door. He was late. He had sounded so nice on the telephone too. But he was very late and Delilah began to feel very stood up. Stood up by no ordinary man, but a man who was meant to represent all that was honest, decent, and responsible in retail merchandising in Britain. A man she should be able to trust. Her humiliation was nearly complete. She was about to order a drink to assuage her anger when the barman approached, rather officiously she thought. This barman was familiar with women who came in alone, sat alone, didn't order, and watched the door. He ran a reputable establishment and this wasn't good for his business. This was truly monkey-business! "Waiting for someone, Miss?" he asked with a poorly concealed scowl. She was, after all wearing a fake monkey fur. That, in itself, was the very reddest of lights!

Delilah was not in the mood to be subjected to male resentment, not even of any kind. "Yes, as a matter of fact, I am indeed waiting for someone and he is extremely late," she replied haughtily in the most plummy tones she could muster amidst abject humiliation. "If you would be so good, my good man, and bring me two pints of your best bitter and a neat vodka, I should be forever in your debt."

She found her change purse, extracted several banknotes, her last, and tossed them carelessly on the table. "Thank you. My Mother thanks you, my father thanks you, and I thank you. But do be quick about it!" She waved him away. All suspicion banished, he said, "Thank you, Miss."

"That would be," Delilah corrected him, "Ms. Pronounced 'Mizz'!"

This woman could be dangerous thought the barman, returning to the bar to fetch her order. "She might have... connections," he muttered to himself, deciding then and there he would include a compli-mentary snack with her request.

Her drinks arrived accompanied by several multi-coloured gherkins, a largish olive, and a fancy egg-mayonnaise treat surrounded with limp, butter-lettuce. After nearly an hour more everything had been consumed but the neat vodka. Delilah checked her watch and frowned scarily like her mother. Heads would roll!

Of course, she knew there would be nothing of the kind because she was too freaking busy already. She'd not even drawn plans for her freaking, crucial brick wall. She was wasting her time here! She furiously quaffed the vodka, stood up smartly, tugged her fake monkey fur closer, nodded ironically at the barman and charged out of the pub directly into the arms of the running Andrew Atkins.

"Why don't you watch where you're going, monsieur?!" she exclaimed, and teetered tipsily backward on unfamiliar heels.

"Ms. Davies? I'm Andrew Atkins. Delilah Davies?" he said breathlessly, recognizing her from the photo she had enclosed in her letter.

"The very same!" replied Delilah with a great deal, but not all of the pique she had planned to unleash upon this outrageously tardy representative of a respectable, corporate pillar of the community. This traitor to the cause of punctuality. Why not serve up all of her pique? A good question, she asked herself, then answered it: Simply because this man was *gorgeous!* But beware, Delilah! she thought, when men are gorgeous they invariably know it and soon attempt to manipulate. She would not let him know she thought he was gorgeous. It would only make him, on any subsequent date -- if that were in their cards -- even later than he was tonight. And at that time, he would begin to play the power games that gorgeous men inevitably play with overly patient, comely women like herself. Women who were not beautiful but err...only comely. But that was all right with her. 'Comely' had served her well enough. She was comfortable in these shoes. Well, not exactly comfortable in *these* treacherous, high-heeled shoes but comfortable in shoes in general. Why had she drunk so fucking, freaking much?!

"Sorry I'm late," he said, "Is that a fake monkey fur you're wearing?"

"What if it is?" Delilah was cross. Not for being only err... comely, but because she was so aware of it because he was so gorgeous. He was also, she was certain, even after her couple of pints and a neat vodka, as aware of her being only comely as she of was of him being simply gorgeous. And gorgeous always trumped comely. And he knew it. How dare he for being so fucking late! Two pints of best bitter and a neat vodka assured her that his tardiness was an abomination! Still...

"We've had some fake-fur ideas recently. I wonder if you'd care to discuss them with me?" he said engagingly, and consequently became suddenly more gorgeous whilst she remained only comely. A bitter pill, might Mum have said whilst high on poetry.

"Are you quite certain you can spare the time?" Delilah replied icily, thinking he must apologise at least once more before she could...

"I am so very sorry I was late. It was unavoidable. Come in and let me get you a drink," he said, still catching his breath.

Now, only a bit aloof because, after all, gorgeous was gorgeous, Delilah said, "I've had a drink. I've had three drinks and..."

All this, still at the pub entrance.

Andrew Atkins gently took her arm. "Come in with me, please, Ms Davies."

They went in. At their table, he said "What are you having?"

"White wine, she said grandly, "I've a positive pass-sion for white wine this even-ning."

Andrew Atkins' registered only slight surprise at Delilah's odd demeanour and immediately chalked it up to her previous three drinks -- after all he was criminally late.

He went to the bar, returned and set her wine before her, and raised his pint. "Cheers!"

"Cheers," replied fake monkey-furred Delilah, still a bit miffed, or was it the alcohol? She'd have to ask alcohol-familiar Phyllis about that one day. Andrew Atkins was obviously quite taken with her, and Delilah's mood lifted as she noted this intense interest. "He's fascinating," she thought, "but late." Punctuality was, for her, a prime characteristic in a man. Still.

"I'm so sorry," he said again, warming the very cockles of her heart, "Please forgive me. I'm not often late for important engagements."

The man seemed almost to be reading her freaking thoughts!

"What's all this about fake monkey fur?" she asked.

"A lie to get you into that chair. Only prostitutes wear fake monkey fur these days."

Delilah's fuse instantly reignited. Was she that out of touch?! "Then what am I?!" she exclaimed, louder than she'd intended. She was doing that a lot lately. Was it a middle-age thing?

"You are a thing apart," said Andrew Atkins softly and evenly. "Indefinable. You are a wonder, Ms Davies."

This last statement made any serious resentment

of this candid man, who was nearly too glorious to behold, practically impossible. "But you've just said you lied. Am I to believe a liar?" asked Delilah.

"But I am honest about it," replied Andrew Atkins with an unsurpassed, at least in her lifetime, blazing white-toothed grin.

"Ah," she said, "I have met honesty by default."

The ice was broken and they laughed easily. Delilah held up her glass. "Cheers, Andrew Atkins!"

"Cheers, Delilah Davies!"

They toasted and drank and Delilah said "I like your jacket. Very much."

"Good," he said, "That's one of the things I'd thought to discuss with you."

"Fire away!" she said.

Andrew took a pen from one of the many zippered pockets in his jacket, a note pad from another and a pipe and a small pouch of tobacco from yet another. Delilah watched, enchanted.

"It's very practical, isn't it?" said Andrew.

Delilah, who had never met a multi-purposed garment she didn't adore, said "I think it's a splendid design. Hopefully, there will be a woman's line too?"

"What do you think, Delilah?"

"Absolutely. We women need all those pockets to house our hammers and nails." She hadn't missed his dropping the "Ms Davies" which was a relief as it was becoming almost suspicious. Some faux device to keep her off-guard?

Andrew smiled. She returned his smile in aces.

Enlivened, he enthusiastically chatted on, "I've got hidden pockets too. Several of them. I'm not even sure where all of them are. Actually, this jacket is the reason I'm so late. I had to find it in stock. It's not yet out and I wanted your opinion on it."

"My *informed* opinion?"

"Indeed," he smiled, "your informed opinion."

"You smoke a pipe, I see."

"Yes. Would you mind?"

"You'll get cancer of the lip in a minute."

"Will I?" he laughed.

"My uncle smoked a pipe. He got cancer of the lip. May I have another white wine, please? As we are about to discuss clothing, I'm certain it would loosen my facilities."

Loose facilities were always a plus and Andrew Atkins seemed more than happy to comply. Delilah was no longer suspicious. She smiled, he smiled. Their contact was warm, innocent, and as light as it was refreshing. At last, mused Delilah, as Andrew went to the bar to replenish their drinks, at last, I've met my equal in high principles and sincere sensibilities. She watched approvingly as he returned and sat. She would have got the drinks herself but these goddamned heels made her more than a bit unsteady. She loved Andrew's shiny black hair -- what an uplifting change after, what was his name? Oh, yeah. Far-too young, ginger Tom. Still...

"Thanks," she said, jettisoning that unfortunate young pseudo cowboy whom she was joyfully certain would have his seventeen-year-old muscular arms full with his devious Debbie character. So, exulting in her good fortune, Delilah raised her white wine and said "Cheers, Andrew!"

"Cheers," he said, as delighted with her as she was with him.

They drank and simultaneously sighed.

Delilah said, sighing again, "I adore lots of pockets. You never know what you'll find in a pocket, n'est-ce pas?"

"That has been my experience of the world as well," added Andrew. "One simply never knows."

Delilah drove into her semi-commercial mews noting that yet another business had become a very smallish, very stylish, private home. She'd had two coffees before they left the pub and was quite capable of driving. Andrew followed in his electric car -- yet another solid plank in his edifice -- an ecologically conscious man. No sooner had they gone into Delilah's house and Andrew was attempting to get his bearings in this, her puzzling 'work in progress' as she had described it, when the doorbell rang and Joanna, sobbing, rushed in. "My Darren's left me!" she cried, throwing herself into Delilah's arms. Then, as suddenly: "You must be the famous Andrew Atkins."

"Hardly famous," he said, "But hello, anyway." He offered his hand to shake and she shook it.

"Hello," said Joanna, wiping her eyes.

"This is my next door neighbour and dear old friend, Joanna," said Delilah, smoothing Joanna's lovely dark hair as she nestled into the sanctuary of Delilah's embrace. "I've known her since she was a child. Her Darren has apparently just left her."

"So I've heard," said Andrew.

"He left his son with me too. Little Mikie."

"Oh?" said Andrew, able in a trice to reassure.

"Yes, he did," moaned Joanna, reassured by his able reassurance, but adding, "Not sure I can cope."

"Yes, you will. I'm certain you will," said Andrew, being certain of nothing more than that Joanna's relationship was far from a sure thing and he'd only met one of the two involved.

"Oh! Do you really think so?" said Joanna.

"Yes he really thinks so, Jo!" said Delilah, who grinned at Andrew over Joanna's head, "Though he is a self-confessed liar. Aren't you, Andrew?"

"All men are liars!" shot out Joanna, ripping

herself from Delilah's comforting embrace. "Darren's a liar too!"

"Hell's ballocks!" said Delilah, "I've met two women today, both crying over men. Oh yes, plus my Mum who makes me cry. What does that say about the female gender, Andrew?"

"That you're all the same?" He laughed and held up his hands in defence against the humorous glares of both women. "Joke, ladies! Joke!"

"Andrew is here, Jo, to watch me model..."

"Is he?" murmured Joanna, taut with sorrow for herself.

"Yes," continued Delilah, "an ensemble to illustrate the point of my recent letter on the subject."

"Is he indeed? I wouldn't trust men as far as I could throw 'em!" warned Joanna. "Especially if they've got little children they leave on your doorstep like Darren left little Mikie. He's sleeping now, that poor, little fatherless child."

The doorbell rang. Delilah shrugged hopelessly at the disaster her evening with Andrew had already become, and opened the door. Mandy came rushing in. "Delilah! Thank God you gave me your address! Can I stay here tonight?! Trevor is harassing me at my Mum's. I sneaked out the back door. He keeps tooting that horn on his Jaguar! I hate that Jaguar even if it is bronze! It has the loudest horn of any car I know!"

"My Mum loves it," said Delilah.

"She can have it!" spat Mandy.

"I wish she could," said Delilah. "I'd teach her to drive somewhere far away. This is Joanna, Mandy, and this is Andrew. I was about to do some modelling for Andrew."

"Gosh, kiddo," said Mandy, " I didn't know it was as bad as all that. No wonder you wanted your fake monkey fur back. I could loan you a few quid. I raided Trevor's pockets yesterday. Anyhow, I was once into modelling myself and I know what it means."

"I thought you might," said Delilah.

"Whaddaya mean by that then?" replied Mandy.

"Nothing. But thanks for the loan offer. This is Mandy, everyone. She's just left my ex-husband, Trevor."

"Good for you, Mandy!" cried Joanna, "I've known Trevor since I was a kid. He's a proper bastard!"

"No he's not. I just don't like him anymore," said Mandy.

"Good for you!" said Joanna, "He's an old harasser. All men are! Ask Delilah. Trevor's just like Darren. He can't keep it in his pants and he can't be trusted! Delilah, did I ever tell you about..."

"Joanna!" said Delilah, "Have you been drinking, love?"

Joanna ignored her, said "But at least Trevor

didn't leave a child on my doorstep."

Mandy gave Joanna an odd look, said "Why would he do that?"

"That was Joanna. This is Andrew," said Delilah quickly, "He's in middle-management at Marks and Sparks and I was harassing *him*."

"Oh, is that what you mews-types call it?" said Mandy.

"That may not be what you call it but it's what I call it," said Delilah sweetly but firmly.

"Fair enough, love," said Mandy. "To each his own. Where do I bed down? It's late."

"I was just thinking the same thing myself," said Delilah.

Joanna shuffled pitifully to Mandy. "My Darren left me tonight."

"Tough luck, kid," said Mandy.

"He left his little five-year-old son, Mikie, with me too. I think he's five. He looks five." Joanna slapped away several large tears and moaned "Don't know if I can cope."

"You'll manage, love," said Mandy gently, having time and again been there herself.

Joanna was pleased, batted away more tears. "Will I?"

"Sure, honey. It's written all over you," said Mandy.

"Is it, really?! How?"

"Right here." With her finger, Mandy wrote and spoke "Success with a capital S" across the extremely pleased Joanna's forehead, then turned to Delilah, said "Bed?"

"Here, I'm afraid. The rock-hard sofa," said Delilah.

"Oh!" exclaimed Mandy, "I get to sleep on a chesterfield. My old granddaddy used to smoke 'em."

"I should get back," said Joanna, "Mikie's sleeping."

"Yes, Jo. Go. I'll talk to you in the morning."

Joanna, leaving, paused by the door, swiped a finger across her forehead. "Success! Thank you, Mandy. Maybe it will help me get a job too. I'm unemployed. Delilah's fault. She told me not to..."

"Goodnight, Jo," said Delilah, Mandy and Andrew almost simultaneously. Joanna left, happily waving to all.

"Sweet kid," said Mandy and dropped herself on the chesterfield sofa and immediately began to remove her stockings. "I hate stockings. Trevor loved stockings. I wear stockings to please Trevor. I hate Trevor. No, I don't. Yes I do."

"Go ahead, Mandy, hate Trevor if you must," said Delilah, "Many do. Release your unique woman within."

"Okay," said Mandy and unzipped her skirt.

She's very suggestible thought Delilah, steering Andrew safely away through the crude remains of the hall.

"What about tomorrow?" said Andrew.

"Yes. Tomorrow is another day."

"I'll ring you?"

"Oh yes."

"Yes it is then?" said Andrew.

"Yes," smiled Delilah, "Most certainly, yes."

"Then yes it is."

Mandy plodded out in her underwear. "Got any blankets, kids?"

Delilah found a blanket in a cupboard, thrust it at Mandy, and glanced longingly at Andrew, who said "Goodnight, then."

Delilah saw him to the door. "Goodnight, sweet prince," she said recklessly, because it seemed such a perfect thing to say just then. But in the next moment she mercilessly accused herself of foolishness, of weakness, even as she and Andrew lingered longingly at the door. Was she or was she not a paradoxical disaster? She'd only just met the man.

"Goodnight to you, sweet princess," said Andrew, and threw her a kiss.

"Look, you two!" yelled Mandy from the end of the hall, "I gotta get me some Z's! I'm a bee-atch without my beauty sleep! Can you get this over with, one way or another?!"

Delilah, in a bliss-mist, closed her door after him, leaned her ear against it to hear as Andrew's car started and departed. But there was only silence. Then she remembered he had an Eco-friendly electric car. What a man! He was gorgeous and he drove Eco-Electric! And he worked for Marks and Sparks! Who could ask for anything more? Phyllis's good luck shilling was working overtime. But was Delilah becoming another woefully uncritical woman? A woman caught in a Joanna ziz-zag? A woman who'd suffer anything for the man she loved?

"He's a dish, that Andrew Atkins," called Mandy, tucking herself under her lightly plaster-dusted blankets. "He's gorgeous, but is he married?"

Dreamily, Delilah murmured, "I never thought to ask." He was the right age, late thirties -- early forties, silky unretouched black hair, a decent build, what she had seen of it, and an intelligent, cultured demeanour which didn't depend upon a knowledge of the violin or anything even marginally highbrow. But who did she think she was, anyhow? Einstein? Her with her scrawny claims to culture, clinging to a few month's mediocre piano lessons an eon ago -- its towering achievement being her startling repertoire: The Scarf Dance and Rustles of Spring, both in simplified beginner's versions. Come off your cloud, Delilah, dismount from that high horse. Just because you taught Art once, at college-level who the hell do you think you are?! You're no Clara Schumann, or Mary Cassatt, or even Paloma Picasso! To top it off you're only comely, not gorgeous! So why are you fucking about with these impossible standards you demand from everyone else?

Yeah! Okay! For chrissake! Leave it! shouted her woman within. So she left it.

Delilah's moment of doubt then passed without terminal consequences. She made her way back through her tangled makeshift hallway, climbed the makeshift stairway to her makeshift bedroom and dropped on her bed, where she asked herself sotto voce, "But is he married?"

She would think about that tomorrow.

It was tomorrow and Delilah was still thinking about Andrew Atkins as she scraped away the blackest bits of several slices of burnt morning toast into the kitchen sink. Joanna sat on the two sacks of cement by the shipping-crate-built table, sipping coffee. "Why is this cement so hard?" she asked plaintively.

"Because it is cement," answered Delilah patiently.

"Oh," replied Joanna.

"Also, it got rained on and is set solid. It is like sack-shaped carved rock, heavy as an ancient aqueduct. I was going to move 'em and it's impossible. I hated those thrift-shop kitchen chairs I bought and sent back. But these cement sacks were free. They're something to sit on for the moment."

"Darren's wife came for Mikie this morning," said Joanna.

"So you said, love, several times."

"But I didn't tell you that Mikie cried, did I?" continued Joanna. "He didn't want to go with her because he doesn't like her. And he doesn't like her because he knows -- children sense these things -- he knows that she doesn't like him. So he cried."

"How do you know, Joanna, really know, that Mikie's mother doesn't like him?"

"Because Darren the bastard said so."

"And you believe him?"

"All men are liars! But Mikie's Mum did look as if she liked him. I will admit that. I will rethink it."

"Good," sighed Delilah, still attempting to contemplate life before the advent of Andrew Atkins, a man whose brain she was, worryingly, beginning to feel comfortable with. "Then that's settled."

"I suppose she does like Mikie," said Joanna, "But I don't like her. And I still don't have a job."

"You've only one mouth to feed now, love. Your

own. That's an improvement, isn't it? "

"If you say so, Delilah. God, Darren is a bastard! Just when we were beginning to cope too! That bastard! What do you think of Andrew Atkins?"

"He's all right. For middle-management," said Delilah, revealing nothing.

"I wouldn't mind him managing my middle," said Joanna, brightening for a moment.

Delilah was unwilling to admit something of such importance to anyone before her woman within had sufficiently considered it. Particularly now, because Delilah knew that she herself, was doing a bum job. She was too involved too soon with not even a definitive kiss from Andrew to gage her progress. She tossed some scraped toast on a dish before Joanna.

"It's burnt, what do you think of Mandy?" said Joanna taking a bite of scraped, past-it, toast.

"I like her."

"I like her too. She's very positive, isn't she, Delilah?"

"She's got "success" written right across her forehead," mused Delilah, her mind on Andrew Atkins, and not willing to be lightly wrenched away.

"Oh, d'you think so?"

"Yes," replied Delilah, almost sternly.

Joanna was delighted. "Just like me!"

"Not precisely," said Delilah, "But she's on her way -- she's gone back to Trevor." Delilah's irony was invisible to Joanna -- one of the reasons Delilah had always liked her. Because Delilah had never seemed too sarcastic for dear Jo. This was a comfort, particularly after one of Mum's tempestuous overnights. Mum was the mistress of irony, as well as, by her instructor's proclamation, the phenomenon of evening poetry, and lately, Delilah's unsolicited moral protector. For at least a month Mum's benighted evening class had been mired in metaphor. Surely there was poetry without metaphor? Delilah knew nothing about poetry. She only knew what she liked.

"Your Trevor is a bastard," said Joanna.

"Joanna, love, he has not been my Trevor for a year. Not before, either. Ever. Not after our three day honeymoon in Brighton during which...fuck it," she said, and the floodgates opened. "Our denouement was ten gruelling years. It took that long for me to pull my head out of my arse. Men are different from us. What ever was I thinking of for ten gruelling years?"

"Sorry," said Joanna. "He's a bastard anyway."

"Darling, don't get your knickers in a twist. No one is all bad. Not Trevor. Not me. Not even Nigel," said Delilah though Nigel was the only person on earth that Delilah truly did loathe. "Trevor, however, changes when he sees a fuckable prospect or he gets behind the wheel of his Jaguar. Did you hear him? Last night? Tooting his freaking horn for Mandy? It went on for a full half hour before she went back to him."

"As you well know, Delilah, I don't hear anything after I've had my hot milk. I'm out like a light. God! these cement sacks are hard."

"Have a hot milk," said Delilah.

"Never fails," said Joanna. "God, these cement sacks are hard."

"They are too heavy to move," answered Delilah by rote, thinking again about Andrew. Was she in love at last? Or only horny? I hope it's only horny, the ruling lechery in her insisted. Love was too complicated to consider with lust ascendant. But, qualitatively, how then, did she differ from Trevor in pursuit of the fuckable? Well, being unmarried, her escalator antics were not bound by sacred vows... Oh, forget it! A night of delirious abandonment was required before sane judgment on any subject.

That night, in the dark, bedclothes rustled. "Hell's ballocks," exclaimed Delilah, "They were right here! In this drawer! In a nice plump envelope. Mum must have taken them again!"

Andrew said "I errr...came prepared."

"Oh jolly good!" cried Delilah, "Then we can get right on with it. Ballocks! This is so unromantic."

"It's in one of our new jacket's hidden pockets. I'm not precisely sure which one," said Andrew.

Delilah replied "We'd better turn on the light then. Ballocks! This is so freaking unromantic."

The bedlamp went on. Andrew rolled out of bed, said "My jacket's downstairs," threw Delilah's awful chenille robe over his shoulders and was out the door. After a moment there was a crash. Delilah sprang up and rocketed down the stairs and found Andrew holding his toe and huddling on the floor. He'd blundered into the unforgiving sacks of cement.

"God, I'm sorry!" said Delilah.

"Can you fetch my jacket?" he said, "it's over there. I don't think I can walk quite yet."

"Of course. God, I'm so sorry," said Delilah. She snatched his jacket off the sofa and assisted him up the stairs into the bedroom.

"It's in our super-secret, mugger-proof pocket," said Andrew as he limped, with Delilah's gentle support, to the bed, and sat and began, in near frenzy, to unzip pocket after pocket. "I'd better check all of them just to make sure!"

"Yes, love," said Delilah, "check all of them just to make sure."

"I think the super-secret pocket is in this seam...

somewhere." He struggled with the seam. "No. Not here. Damn!"

"Damn!" said Delilah, a beacon of support for this toe-damaged, could she say 'Hero' yet? With impunity? Yes she could! He had the patience of Solomon. As well as the face and physique of Adonis, which was, of course, enough in itself. For a while. Her woman within would undoubtedly agree, lust ascendant or not. But she'd also applaud Delilah's patience. And Delilah's strength of purpose and her resourcefulness under pressure. "Maybe it's on the other side," Delilah said helpfully, "Other side, same seam?"

Andrew struggled with the seam at the other side, said "No. Damn!"

"Damn," sighed Delilah, and whispered, "This is so unromantic."

"No! Wait! exclaimed Andrew, "I remember! It's just under the lining at the back!" He straightened the lining at the back, found and unzipped a pocket. "Damn!"

"Not there?" said Delilah.

"No. Damn," said Andrew.

"Damn," said Delilah.

"But that wasn't the super-secret, mugger-proof pocket!" Andrew was elated.

"Oh?" asked Delilah.

"No!" he said, "That was only one of the two ordinary super-secret pockets!"

"Oh. An ordinary super-secret pocket, was it?!"

"Uh-huh. What I'm looking for is the super-secret, mugger-proof, water-tight pocket. It's the very toughest to find."

"Apparently," sighed Delilah.

"A lot of planning went into it," said Andrew, his eyes glowing with pride.

"It seems a grand success," said Delilah.

Andrew was pleased with this lovely woman's assessment. "Yes, it is, isn't it?"

"Between my Mum and Marks and Sparks we seem to be doomed to a life apart. I fear my attempts to harass middle-management have come to naught."

"If this is harassment, may I have some more, please?" replied Andrew and laughed. Delilah joined him and they laughed until, from just below the bedroom window came the inebriated, familiar slur, of Phyllis.

"Do I hear a party in progress? Delilahhhh! Oh, Delilahhh! Phyllis, here! Delilah, come out and play!"

"Hell's ballocks!" cried Delilah and stuck her head out the window.

"Go home, Phyllis, you'll hurt yourself. If you don't, I might. Go home, dear! We'll talk tomorrow."

"No, we won't! I don't want to go home! I wanna

talk now!"

Phyllis was dressed to the hilt with a lovely feather fluttering on a black band precisely over the middle of her forehead. She was weaving only slightly. She looked a knockout.

"I have got company, dear!" yelled Delilah with an anxious glance at Andrew.

"I don't care! I don't care!" sang Phyllis in her best whisky contralto.

"I have got com-pan-ny!" repeated Delilah.

"Then have some more, sweetie, have some more!" Laughed Phyllis who now began to pound on Delilah's front door.

"If you'll drive her home, Andrew, I'll see if I can find a what's-it at Joanna's."

"A deal!" said Andrew offering his hand, and they shook.

"How'd it go?" said Delilah when Andrew returned.

"Not bad," said Andrew. "She's all right, really. She wanted to pay me."

"Christ! She thought you were a taxi?"

"Not exactly." He smiled then laughed. "But I was flattered. How'd it go with you?"

"Success!" sang Delilah.

"Jolly good," said Andrew who began to undress

when a car screeched up just below the bedroom window and tooted. Delilah rushed to her window. It was Trevor's bronze Jaguar. "Come out, Mandy!" he yelled, "I know you're in there! Make her come out, Delilah! You put her up to this!"

"Go home, Trevor!" called Delilah whose spirit was sinking rapidly. What would Andrew think? What would any sane man think? "That I'm a nutter?" she murmured. Andrew heard her and had thought just that. But didn't mind. This comely woman was... was simply surreal.

"I won't go home until you've given me Mandy!" shouted Trevor. "This is your fault, Delilah! Tell Mandy to come out!"

"Mandy is not here!"

"Shall I fix his face for him?" announced Andrew, rising defiantly, "I was medium-weight champion at college."

"No, darling," said Delilah, and Andrew, momentarily satisfied with the 'darling', sat peacefully back on the bed but did begin to wonder. Still...

"Tell her I love her!" pleaded Trevor, tooting his horn and shouting desperately, "Mandy, baby!"

"She is not freaking here!" yelled Delilah.

There was more horn tooting and windows slammed open in the mews pouring out mild expletives. Among them, Joanna's. "Go away, Trevor, you bastard!" Trevor had now become Joanna's stand-in scumbag for her disappeared Darren.

Trevor tooted his car horn again, yelling "Mandy!" over and over until his voice morphed to sobs.

"Stop that, Trevor!" cried Delilah. "Be a man!"

"Make him go away, Delilah! I can hardly cope as it is!" yelled Joanna.

"You never could cope, Joanna!" sobbed Trevor. "Everybody knows it!"

"Trevor, please!" called Delilah, "Joanna is one of our oldest friends!"

"You are desecrating my sleep, Trevor!" yelled Joanna.

"Have a hot milk!" sobbed Trevor.

"Have a hot milk, Joanna! It'll help, love!" yelled Delilah.

"Have a hot milk, Joanna," shouted someone from across the mews.

"I can't cope, Delilah! I can't cope!" cried Joanna.

"She never could cope, Delilah!" sobbed Trevor. "You never could cope, Joanna!"

"Please go home, Trevor!" called Delilah.

Andrew Atkins sat quietly, checked his watch, and wondered some more. Then a bit more, and began, quietly, to pull on his socks.

"I will not go home! Not till you give me my Mandy!" sobbed Trevor.

Delilah leaned out of her window and shook her fist at the bronze Jaguar. "Mandy is not here! I have company! Com-pan-ny! So leave us alone and go home! Please!"

"No!" sobbed Trevor. "I won't! I won't!"

"Go home, Trevor!" shouted someone from across the mews.

"Yeah, Trevor! Go home, goddamn it!" cried someone else.

Delilah's front door opened softly and Andrew, not noticed by Delilah or Trevor, crept out, tiptoed into his car, and headlights off, still unnoticed and powered by his blessed eco-batteries, slipped slowly, silently out of the mews.

Trevor, Delilah, Joanna and the occasional enraged mews neighbour, continued to trade insults as Nigel's back door opened and his dog trotted out for a bit of pissing mischief. It ran directly across the little dividing garden to Delilah's potted lilac. There, to Nigel's delight, it cocked its leg, peed and ran glee-fully back to Nigel who, smiling, closed his door quietly and sat back to enjoy the high energy fiasco next door.

Delilah was not aware of Andrew Atkin's depar-ture for twenty minutes. Or more.

4

DELILAH STRIKES OUT
IN A TOTALLY NEW DIRECTION

It was time to face the music. Since her divorce settlement, a year before. Delilah had lived in self-inflicted,
much reduced circumstances. She could have asked
for far more and got it but she wouldn't and didn't.
Her outsized sense of justice and fair play invariably
favoured the other person at her own expense. It was
a weakness about which she often wrangled with her
woman within.

Delilah had, the year before, also cast off her
mobile telephone and deserted her time-consum-
ing, online computer in the interests of solitude and
budget. But living like a pauper for her pottery had
severe disadvantages that could not be rationalized
away. Her year as a single and her sluggish pottery
business and her money-guzzling new home -- relic of

a shoebox that it was -- demanded more money. A lot more money. It was time Delilah got real, announced her concerned alter ego. This time Delilah listened to her better self, this unique woman within. She had no choice.

Delilah and Mum sat over cups of coffee at the furthermost corner table in the St. Pancras railway caf. As they waited for Mum's train, Delilah concentrated on a paperback with a lurid cover illustration of a statuesque, scantily-clothed woman towering over the title, 'She, Who Knew Perfectly Well What She Wanted.'

Mum, scowling, was attempting to scrape the extra-thick, sugary icing from an iced bun.

"She's done it again. Delilah! She knows I don't like the thick, overly sugared ones. I've told her often enough."

Delilah muttered "I'm sure you have," and read on.

"Delilah? I say she's done it again!"

Delilah, without looking up from her book, said "Done what, Mum? Who... has... done... what?"

Mum held up the iced bun. "My iced bun has got too much icing on it!"

"Then take it back." Delilah continued reading.

"I can't!" protested her mother.

Without looking up, Delilah said "Why not?"

"Because I've scraped all the icing off it! That's why not!"

"Well done, darling! Then eat it. It's got no icing on it," said Delilah and returned to her lurid paperback.

Mum gave Delilah a look of terrible wrath and moaned.

Delilah continued to read, muttered "Then what's the freaking problem?"

Mum began, sullenly, to nibble at her abused iced bun. "The problem... the problem is getting old. We're not taken serious. It's not just iced buns, my girl. It's the general predicament of we, the aged. First our eyes go. Then it's our knees, hips, elbows, and ears." Mum took a dainty sip of coffee. "Then..."

"Then it's your iced buns. I've problems of my own, Mum."

"...Then it's our children. Our children who profess to love us!"

Delilah looked up from her book and grinned, "When have I ever professed that, darling?"

"Why don't you just chop off my head and throw me in a ditch!" moaned her mother.

"I won't lie. It had crossed my mind."

"What sort of problems, Delilah?" insisted Mum. "What sort of problems could a young-*ish* woman like you have?"

Delilah dropped her paperback on the table, took a swallow of coffee and a glass of water for a chaser and grimly proceeded. "My kiln is bust. Both kilns as a matter of fact, are bust! I cannot fire and glaze the smiling frogs or curly-tailed piglets, my most popular lines. Without firing and glazing they cannot be sold and if they cannot be sold I am without income and if I am without income I cannot afford cement for my garden goddesses or the foundation for my brick wall or..."

"The myriad Fates have offered you a choice!" announced Mum, suddenly become a joyous example of her poetry instructor's opinion. He had called her a phenomenon. She would live up to that and reclaim her errant daughter through lyrical chat. "Stop messing about, Delilah, and go back to Trevor!"

Mum snatched Delilah's paperback from her, glanced at it and glowered malevolently. "And stop reading this filth!"

"Fortunately, dear, to get over the rough patches, I have a little set-by," said Delilah, "Possibly just enough for another kiln."

"Trevor's got a lot set by," said Mum. "I have it from Joyce Grudden that your Trevor has begun serious excavations for a heated swimming pool."

"Now," continued Delilah who hadn't heard a

word, "the question is, do I spend what little I've got set-by on a new kiln and continue with my pottery business?"

"Which has been a terrible failure from the start," added Mum, "A horrific failure, a disaster."

"Said my mother, encouragingly... Or shall I," Delilah went on slowly, deep in thought, "Or shall I strike out in a totally new direction?"

"You've been striking out in far too many directions for any normal person, let alone a proper lady of the community."

"To use good old American baseball lingo, I've certainly been striking out."

Delilah went back to her lurid-covered paperback.

"Your Trevor and his pleasant woman are having their problems," said Mum, with narrow-eyed glee. "And Trevor told me to warn you to stay out of his affairs d'coeur." Mum was proud of that one! She had scored again. In French!

"Now is the time to strike, darling! When he's all askew! When his pleasant woman..."

"Her name is Mandy."

"When his pleasant woman," continued Mum, "is making his life a Living Hell!"

"They're making my life a hell too," said Delilah, "the both of them. They're children." Delilah threw down her book. "Mum. I have decided to strike out in a totally new direction!"

Mum, disgusted, glared at her. Delilah held up her paperback. "Adult literature. Written by a woman for women. But with a difference. Vintage adult literature. Erotica from the recent past, a scantily clad trip down memory lane for discerning women!"

"In other words, filth for the middle-aged elite!" spat Mum, who began to delicately nibble the last of her disappointing bun.

"Time for your train, love," sighed Delilah, averting her eyes from Mum's tiny, deeply irritating munches.

As Delilah helped Mum aboard her train, Mum shivered, reached into her coat pocket for her silk 'emergency' scarf and got more than she bargained for. The plump envelope of condoms shot out from where she had hidden and forgotten it. It seemed, this horrid plump envelope, to have an uncanny life of its own and bounced away as Mum angrily tried to snatch it up. But Delilah was too fast for her, grabbed the plump envelope, glowered at Mum, and stuck it into her own jacket pocket.

As the train pulled away, Mum frowned and sat steely in her seat, refusing to wave goodbye or look at Delilah. Delilah waved goodbye anyway. After all, her Mum was her Mum and she loved her unconditionally. Delilah knew that we all got old much sooner than we'd reckoned and when the time came, she, Delilah, might inadvertently tax the patience of far too many Good Samaritans before she was pushing up her own metaphorical daisies.

It was decision time. Delilah would now strike out in a totally new direction. To this end and at her wit's end, Delilah sat at her ex-shipping-crate slash kitchen table before Mum's ancient mechanical typewriter. The decision was made: Delilah's only software was now herself, and her only hardware, this typewriter and the escalators of the world.

Delilah's pursuit of the sensible, cultured, possibly violin-case carrying male would now play twofold into her totally new direction. One: for her own sexual needs as required; and Two: raw material for her money-making Adult Literature by a woman, and for women.

Delilah was poised to create a world where yobbos and ill-natured males were simply ignored and her worthy women experienced ecstasy on a daily basis with the responsible, sensible, sensitive, Adonis-like men they deserved. Delilah's novel would be as gripping as 'She, Who Knew Perfectly Well What She Wanted'.

Through Delilah's pages, would pulse the

amorous odyssey of Sybil, a woman of a certain age, of tantalizing beauty, energy, a delicious sense of humour, a kind heart and endless moral fibre. A single woman who never, in the past, said no but never said yes either -- a titillating, erotic enigma of towering proportions!

Delilah had already chosen her nom de plume, 'Lascivia Lyscentia', which slid lazily off the tongue-in-cheek, in a manner of speaking. All that was required was the lecherous enthusiasm of Lascivia's née Delilah's readers. This, Delilah was convinced, would lead to bags of money. She knew she could do it. Why? Because it had become her raison d'être, and the French were infallible in matters of the heart -- and other pertinent organs. Metaphorically speaking, of course.

Delilah, in her inimitably eccentric way, her sluttish spirits aroused, would soon sashay down the primrose path of decadence with a difference. Vintage decadence, it had to be. Authentic erotic decadence was rare as hen's teeth in the present world of anything goes. Where, today, was the exquisitely libidinous turn of phrase, the eloquent excitement of gorgeous and/or comely bodies slamming rhythmically together in perfect bliss? Where indeed? Delilah must set the stage anew. Thank God she was thirty-nine and familiar with the recently old and comfortingly cosy!

As she typed, Delilah kept an eye out, through her kitchen door, for Nigel's loathsome dog but was soon lost in the pleasure of her work and spoke as she typed, spoke for a more dramatic effect:

> Sybil Sanford, sublimely con-
> fident, sat sleepily spread-
> eagled on fine, clipped grass
> in the high summer sunshine
> of St. James's Park gazing
> with total satisfaction at
> her own gorgeous legs...

Delilah sighed with pleasure, took a slurp of strong coffee and glared at the rat-dog, as it crept perilously close to her side of the garden. She watched for a moment but was soon engaged in her stylish smut and continued to type, intoning as she wrote.

> Suddenly Sybil was aware of
> a figure beside her. Not sur-
> prisingly, considering her
> scant attire, it was the fig-
> ure of a young man, ebony-
> haired and clad in the tight-
> est of jeans, the bulging

crotch of which...

Delilah chuckled, continued.

...the bulging crotch of
which, shamelessly celebrated
his glorious --

Delilah paused, thought it, got it, and typed:

rising maleness...

Nigel's dog, unnoticed by Delilah, cocked its leg
and peed on her half-dead, potted lilac.

But Delilah saw nothing. She was exulting in the
new power of her metaphorical pen -- the mechanical
typewriter!

Sybil's sharp eyes stared in
sweet wonder at this fetching young male. She began to
float like white froth on a
soon-to-break wave. She soon
found herself powerless!
A slave to something much
larger, she fervently hoped,
than herself...

Delilah stopped typing, clapped her hands. Through the kitchen door she saw that Nigel's dog seemed a safe distance from her sacred lilac. So, in the creative throes of striking out totally anew, sugar plums of instant wealth dancing in her head, she continued.

> With a resounding riiiiip! the lovely young man's zipper was torn asunder and thrust skyward was the sleekest, shapeliest...

"Darren's left me!" wailed Joanna who had spotted Delilah through the kitchen door and was frantically pounding on it. "Delilah! Darren's left me!"

"I know, love," called Delilah who rose patiently from her typewriter and comforted the stricken Joanna into her kitchen slash office. "But that was last week, wasn't it?"

"He came back, Delilah!" sobbed Joanna, "He came back and left again! Sod him! Just now! Just this minute!"

"Why the rotten egg! You're better off without him," said Delilah, gently placing Joanna -- to spare her from hardened cement sacks -- on a folding chair found in another recently discovered closet. "What has he ever done for you?"

"He loved me, Delilah! He loved me! But you wouldn't know about love!" sobbed Joanna.

"Wouldn't I?" replied Delilah with some feeling.

Joanna checked herself. "No, I meant you wouldn't care if somebody left you. Twice, even. In one week. Because you're strong!" Joanna began again to wail.

"I suppose you'll be wanting tea now that Darren's left you, twice?" said Delilah.

Joanna wiped her eyes, brightened. "I wouldn't say no. I used the last of my tea-milk for..."

"I understand completely," replied Delilah, cutting her off. She clicked on the electric kettle, and began to set a tea tray as Joanna, with an old paint rag, wiped plaster dust from the makeshift table, saw the typewriter and read aloud the paper in it.

"With a resounding riiiiiip! the lovely young man's zipper was torn asunder and thrust skyward was the sleekest, shapeliest..."

Joanna broke off, began to laugh. Delilah frowned and slammed the tea tray on the table. "What's so goddamned funny?!"

Joanna said "What on earth is this?!"

"That's hardly the reaction I expected to my enlightened adult literature written by a woman for women!"

"That's adult literature?" giggled Joanna.

"It is," insisted Delilah.

"Thrust skyward was the sleekest?" Joanna giggled again and choking with laughter, was unable to manage shapeliest.

"My kilns are bust," pleaded Delilah, "I need big money, Joanna, to finish my house. Big money! Now! And there's big money in adult literature by women for women."

"*Sleekest*?" said Joanna, her face streaming with tears of laughter, "*Shapeliest*?!"

"For women of discernment! Women of a certain age! Why not?" cried Delilah.

"With a resounding riiiiip?!" shrieked Joanna, laughing hysterically.

Delilah crumbled and abandoned herself, and the two women, clinging together, laughed helplessly and began to dance, scuffing up tiny joyous puffs of plaster dust from the floorboards of Delilah's has-been but would-be kitchen.

Joanna soon left, incompletely comforted, but full of tea and heavily buttered toast and was at least laughing happily. Alone once again at the kitchen table, her typewriter now primed with Mum's old, but pristine, silk typewriter ribbon, Delilah threw herself into the vintage arena of her noveau literature; The recent past. This first episode would explore the secret, not so very long ago, underbelly of London

Transport, when genial female conductors with shining ticket machines round their necks roamed the aisles of tidy, red double-decked London buses. Stories one would blush to hear! Surely, there must be individuals of both genders, reasoned the newly christened Lascivia Lyscentia, individuals of insight and intelligence who still blushed?

SYBIL LETS HERSELF GO!
Lust On a Red,
Two-Decker London bus.

by

Lascivia

Lyscentia

"Fares? Fares, please?" called Sybil, whose name appeared on a shiny badge over her ample breast, a superb breast, far too shapely and fiercely firm to be an intimate body-part of a woman of fifty-six. She was getting on, but her two perfect bosoms, which had never known the profane touch of a silicone surgeon, apparently didn't know it!

"Sorry," said the first fare of the day, a hot, yet kind, young male who gazed up at Sybil from his lavishly-lashed, dark eyes, and whispered huskily, "To Trafalgar Square. I've only got a fiver. I desperately hope this does not inconvenience you."

"That's alright, love," replied this genial, ravishingly comely conductor who took the fiver, made change, and cranked out the splendid young man's ticket from the impeccably polished chromium ticket machine around her neck. With an innocent smile, she now moved gracefully down the bus aisle calling "More Fares? Fares please?"

Sybil adored her job but was not, she soon realized, completely immune to the white-hot, yet obviously sensitive and caring, persona of this unbelievably gorgeous young man.

At this time in her life
-- not yet sunset, but quite
late afternoon -- Sybil had
long since given up her reckless pursuit of bodily pleasure. It had happened when
her dear mother passed away
whilst she, Sybil, had become
mixed-up and was in the arms
of an undeserving lower type
person under a dampish bridge
in Hackney.

The shock of Mum's death
and Sybil's guilt at not being
at her mother's side in Mum's
time of need, sent Sybil,
sobbing, into a convent of
gentle, caring and devoted
nuns. Several years there-
after she became a waitress
and finally, a proud bus conductor for London Transport.
Her crisply ironed, impeccably laundered uniform, stood
mute testimony to her chaste
and conscientious performance

of all bus-related duties.
Most fortunately, her rapacious sexual appetites had
long ago been vanquished...
or so she thought...

Sybil was simply unbe-
lievably well-preserved for
her age. Her fine, sleek,
glowing skin was still
attractive to men of all
ages and walks of life and
now, to one particular young
man, that kindly, first fare
of the day who now studied
her covertly from the corner
of his lavishly-lashed, dark
eyes. Sybil well knew she
was being covertly studied
by this curly-haired Adonis.
She also knew that, in spite
of her questionable past,
and the inexpressibly awful
heartbreak of the loss of her
beloved Mum, she remained
irresistible, but nonethe-
less had continued to hold
herself back for all these

years. For she dared not wake again the demon passion that even now pulsed pruriently at the blazing core of her being and could so easily be loosed upon an unsuspecting, mass-transit world.

As this young Adonis shyly, though covertly, studied her, he was gob-stopped by her smooth, unusually firm, middle-aged legs! They glowed white-hot through the seeming innocence of her uniform as she loyally sought, above all, for that was the sort of woman she was, to perform her solemn duties for London Transport.

"Mind your step, please. Mind your step, dear," said Sybil kindly, as she gently, lovingly assisted a sweet, white-haired old lady to disembark. This dear, wizened old crone reminded Sybil of her beloved, so tragically departed, mother.

As the day wore on, the young Adonis, who had, incidentally, earlier acquired a London Transport day-pass, continued, still covertly, to watch Sybil from the corner of his eye. This godlike young man was helpless, stirred by a fiery, insistent passion he had never known before. A passion that might well have melted the souls of each and every passenger on the shiny red bus. But now... now the nearly completely tidy bus was empty and parked for the night in the spotless vehicle sanctuary of London Transport.

Ever devoted to her job, Sybil, heroically attempting to ignore this young princeling, was sweeping out the lower deck of her vehicle -- the staff were always encouraged to pitch-in -- The sun was setting and the driver, long gone. But this young Adonis who, pretending to peruse a copy of the Sunday Times, remained in his bus seat, still peering covertly out from under his lushly-lashed lids, still waiting and longing with every fibre of his fiercely fraught being.

Sybil's loyalty to London Transport never faltered and, official broom in her sleek, smooth hands, she swept on. This was her bus and so long as she was its conductor it would be a tidy bus!

Then it happened! As she and her official broom swept nearer, a reckless dart of her eye told her he was like no other, simply like no other! The sun seemed suddenly to set as Sybil's lust suddenly rose! Her astounding inner demon was now rattling at the last gate of her resistance! All the sad lessons of her rapacious past were summarily jettisoned!

"I've had enough of holding myself back!" this gracious, genial, late middle-aged bus conductor hissed through gleaming teeth that were, largely, her own. The young man could only focus on Sybil's fine, sleek, glowing skin as the palpable heat from her unusually firm, hot, middle-aged legs scorched his perfectly smooth complexion like a searing wind over the Sahara! He smouldered a smile and batted his lavishly-lashed lids. Sybil smouldered a smile in return and this proved too libidinously aggravating for the young, but gentle, kind and generous Adonis, who always donated large amounts, when he could afford it, and often at great sacrifice to himself,

to all the major charities,
particularly to a new one:
WOMEN OF A CERTAIN AGE, IN
TROUBLE. This he did each
and every Christmas without
fail. In a trice he was upon
Sybil! "Crikey!" she screamed,
joyously pushing aside her
impeccably polished chromium
ticket machine and throwing
down her specially assigned
London Transport broom, "I
never, never thought it could
be like this!"

"May I help you?" asked the salesclerk at
Commercial Supplies Ltd.

Dazed, Delilah, looked up from a kiln display.
"I'm thinking of two new kilns but I'm not sure I can
afford them."

"We have kilns on special offer this week only,"
said the clerk with a suitable smile.

"Oh?" replied Delilah. It was difficult concentrat-
ing on the task at hand. Her vintage literature had
played in her head for several days now and would
not leave her in peace. She was possessed, as every
creative writer, to survive, must be! So it continued:

The personable salesclerk
eyed the lustrous Sybil with
far more than the sale of one
or even two pottery kilns in
mind. This came as no surprise to Sybil who knew that
her sleek skin always shone
with a certain golden inten-
sity between the hours of
nine and eleven each morning and at the moment it was
only five past ten. Nonethe-
less the salesclerk's obvious
interest caused Sybil's emer-
ald eyes to glitter and her
heart to jump merrily and
her orange-painted nails to
leap to her full, perfectly
sculpted, vermilion lips in
delight! But, not willing to
expose her naked need till
at least ten-thirty when her
cheeks would become reddest
roses in highest summer, she
blushed an astounding pink
and turned demurely away.

Delilah turned demurely away to the puzzlement of the salesclerk who was doing his best to be of assistance.

"We received these high quality kilns in a special purchase and we are passing this advantage on to our customers," he insisted.

Sybil now knew the salesclerk's intentions were focussed on her comeliness alone for she heard that familiar, spasmodic rustle of hardening flesh tussling against his fragrant, freshly pressed trousers. The salesclerk moved closer, quite unaware that he was doing so. There was something mysteriously magnetic about this rainbow of a woman that he would love to put his finger on -- anywhere.

Delilah's glazed expression and her odd tendency to move abruptly into his personal space began to make the salesclerk uneasy.

Suddenly there was a crash of clattering cans, and

Delilah, flung bodily from her erotic literary reverie, discovered that she had backed the poor man over a paint display and now lay awkwardly atop him.

"Oh! I do beg your pardon!!" she cried.

Striking out in a totally new direction had its practical difficulties. If life ever did imitate Art, this was it!

Delilah instantly rolled herself off the dumbfounded salesclerk's abdomen and noticed she had paint on her fingers from the felled display. She reached quickly for a hanky from her jacket and the infamous plump envelope flew out like a frightened magician's dove and burst, scattering its rubbery cargo everywhere. Why had Delilah, after rescuing the condoms from her mother this morning at St. Pancras Station, not removed them from her jacket and placed them back where they belonged, by her freaking bed?!

But there was more to come. The handsome head of her disappeared, almost-lover, Andrew Atkins, now reappeared over a stack of painting accessories as Delilah dropped again to the floor to gather up the many rubbery bits of treasure. This must be done before he recognized her and realized the sublime irony of it all! But now, suddenly, here he was with a small child on each hand and an even smaller one perched like a tiny monkey upon his once seriously admired shoulders.

Delilah, darted about, a hen pecking grain round the floor. She could only grin at Andrew, speechless after her profound near-miss with this gorgeous man who had become oddly unavailable ever since. Were these his brother's children on a shopping tour with their favourite uncle? -- she desperately rationalized. But her moment of fake comfort was suddenly dispelled as she saw Andrew's grossly pregnant wife, who joined him and all those...*children* and sweetly asked "What's all the commotion, darling?"

"So sorry," said Delilah to the gathering crowd of curious shoppers, "I seem to have dropped a day's supply of condoms."

Delilah gazed meaningfully at Andrew, who looked sheepishly away as more shoppers gathered to review the shattered paint display and the condom-pecking Delilah on her knees in the midst of it. Her dazed salesclerk, just rising from the ruin of paint tins, still hoped this eccentric, dishevelled woman might buy two kilns for the price of one -- an incredibly generous offer. But when he saw Delilah marching defiantly towards the door, waving goodbye over her shoulder, his hopes were dashed.

On the bus home Delilah watched a small altercation between two small boys seated opposite.

"You give 'em back!" cried the first boy.

"Won't!" cried the second.

"You will!"

Delilah, fresh from disaster but unscathed was geared up for action with pencil and notepad. So here again in her head was the older, but now, not necessarily wiser Sybil:

"Give him his sweets, love," commanded Sybil, posture-perfect, taut in her London Transport uniform. Sybil, her pert bosoms erect, her ticket machine polished and her senses alert, as ever, to mass-transit injustice wherever she found it, cried "I saw you take his sweeties. Give them back!"

"I shan't!" cried the little bully-boy.

In the throes of her righteous indignation, Sybil expounded, "You will give him back his sweets or remove yourself from this London Transport conveyance!"

"I shan't, I shan't," cried the guilty little bully, who added, "My Pa's in the Mob! Here, Miss, have a jelly-bean."

"I shall not be bribed," cried Sybil, majestically tossing her perfectly gorgeous, silver-grey hair. Still, she reasoned. Still... She did have an uncontrollable sweet-tooth since giving up rampant sex. What difference would a tiny jelly-bean make in the wide wicked world of mass-transit? It was the biggest mistake she would ever make!

Sybil awakened slowly. She knew she had been drugged. Her hands and feet were bound and her lacey black knickers lay crumpled about her sleek ankles. Why oh why had she accepted that jelly-bean? The boy looked innocent enough...

Her bus lurched to a stop and Delilah leapt off. She had big plans. Money-making plans through the power of her pen. But would they coalesce in time? The cold, economically disastrous world of her pottery now intruded.

In her garage slash pottery Delilah wrapped and packed a small row of smiling frogs in a carton for later delivery to a seller. A timid tap at her garage door told her it was Joanna. She sighed, set down a smiling frog and opened the door to the radiantly happy next door neighbour and friend.

"You can stay for five minutes, Jo, I am packing my last order of frogs."

"He's come back!" cried jubilant Joanna, "Darren's come back! He's sleeping!"

"Oh? Did he tire himself eating all the food in your house and leaving a big, oily ring round your bathtub?"

"He's all cuddled in my pillows, like a little boy."

"Darren *is* a little boy."

"Delilah, I had to come over and tell you right away when the iron was hot! I've got a brilliant idea!"

Delilah gave Joanna a blank look, and continued to wrap her smiling frogs.

"Your adult literature, Delilah..." Joanna hesitated then plunged ahead. "You are coming with me tonight! To our writing class. Maybe I can learn to write too, and make a little extra so I can prepare the finer menus that Darren prefers! Isn't it exciting? I enrolled us today! Frankly, Delilah, your adult literature for women leaves much to be desired!"

"That's the idea, isn't it? Much to be desired?" replied Delilah with a half-hearted chuckle, not knowing whether to be elated or discouraged by Joanna's proposition. It would come at a cost, she knew. The cost would be a loss of her, Delilah's, valuable time. Just when she most needed it. Coupled with her new pursuits as a writer, she must soon see to a new roof plus proper walls for every room in her house as well as the removal of those hardened, useless cement sacks. New floors and doors were de rigueur. But where was all the freaking money to come from?!

That wasn't all. She must have decent furniture which she planned to design and build herself but probably never would. She was a beggar who would be a chooser and could never accept the sloppy seconds of anything used and shabby, notwithstanding the ancient chesterfield sofa that, despite the protestations of Mum who remained mum, Delilah was certain she had been born on.

"You inspired me, Delilah! And my Darren thought it was an excellent idea!"

This was the clincher. Anything that Darren, the

master builder thought a good idea, was good enough for Delilah! Her irony again shone for miles. Joanna, as usual, was totally unaware of it. Delilah, as usual, basked in this innocent quality of Joanna's that made Joanna a dearest friend. Of course she would attend the evening writing classes with Joanna. It would make Joanna happy and it could well be a boon to her new direction. And money, lots of it, through her vintage erotica, would be the key to the completion of her dream house and her brick wall.

But Delilah also knew that she was a top-notch builder of never-never dream scenarios. She must get real. Or end up like the previous owner of her miserable little house and garage, Jimmy of Jimmy's Auto Repair. Regardless of Phyllis's change of opinion, was Jimmy really a loser? That question would soon be answered. And more miraculously than anyone could possibly have anticipated. Even Delilah's woman within.

Delilah and Joanna and a plain, very young woman, Melanie, and a nervous young man, Jamie, were seated side by side in the front row of an evening class of about ten students. Their instructor-to-be, Ms Frobisher, would be addressed, she immediately announced, simply as Ondine. But her real name was Ethel, revealed Joanna after a lightning search on her mobile as 'Ondine' consulted her seating chart.

Ondine was an attractive woman of about Delilah's age. She now rose and announced in solemn, stentorian tones: "There is absolutely no substitute for observation. We cannot write accurately about what we do not experience first hand. It is the writer's task to..."

As Ondine continued, Delilah closed her eyes and her natural writer's voice bubbled up and sang in her head.

```
Ethel,   the   evening   school
instructor  was  dedicated  to
sex,  sex,  and  only  sex.  Her
instructor's  role  was  a  cruel
ruse.  She  lured  young  male
hopefuls  with  those  endless
legs  of  hers,  had  her  way
with   these   poor   innocents
then,  sated,  cast  them  aside,
their  young  lives  destroyed.
Her   next   victim   sat   before
her,  drinking  in  her  words
-- Hypnotic  words  that  would
soon  bind  him  in  a  helpless,
inextricable  web  of  passion.
```

The youthful Jamie had proudly announced

to Delilah and Joanna before class that he was also enrolled in his second year of speed reading and writing, and he began taking copious notes and fervently recording every precious word his new instructor uttered. From her provocatively cross-legged position on the edge of her desk Ondine seemed pleased with the youthful, industrious Jamie who had not yet spoken a word.

"And you..." Ondine consulted her seating plan, "Delilah, is it?"

Delilah's eyes blinked open. "What?"

"Your name? Delilah, is it? Shall I simply refer to you as Delilah?"

"Yes, do feel free to simply refer to me thusly, Ethel."

"Ondine will do! What have you, Delilah, to say about observation?"

Delilah muttered "chee-rist! Did I just doze off?"

"What have you to say about Observation?" repeated Ondine gazing glassily at Delilah.

"Well," said Delilah, thinking fast, "Observation? Well. It remains to be seen, doesn't it?"

There was silence in the classroom and no response from anyone but Joanna who was embarrassed for her friend.

"Observation?" said Delilah, weakly. "Remains to be seen? That was a...errr joke."

"Oh, *was* it?" said Ondine, then suddenly, "You!" Like a striking cobra, Ondine consulted her seating plan, "Jamie? What do you think? Re:" She made 'quote' gestures with two fingers of each hand. "Observation?"

Jamie sat up sharply. "We must experience...an experience to errr..."

"Right you are, Jamie. And what about you, Melanie? What are your thoughts on..." up shot Ondine's finger-quotes, "Observation?"

Melanie, melting with embarrassment, said "I only wanted to be an all-round entertainer!" and dissolved into tears.

Ondine gave Melanie a puzzled look and consulted her notepad. "Melanie, are you sure you have enrolled for the right class?"

"Isn't this creative singing and interpretive dancing?" said forlorn Melanie.

"No," replied Ondine, grandly rearing up to defend this fortress of her art. "This is Creative Writing! Perhaps you should have enrolled in Remedial Reading?"

Poor humiliated Melanie had more experience of real life in her little finger than Ethel slash Ondine had in her whole shapely body, including those, those, endless legs, thought Delilah, as Melanie, sniffling, hurriedly left the room to re-enroll. Good luck to her! Creative writing? Bunkum! Taught by a rank amateur who spoke rubbish! Delilah vowed that this was to be her last few minutes with Ethel who seemed to lack a crucial requisite any instructor of creative writing must have, a freaking sense of humour and... most important of all, The Milk of Human Kindness! Delilah and Joanna, who felt the same, left at the first break, never to return.

"Ethel had no sense of humour," said Delilah the next afternoon.

Joanna said, "I agree," as she entered Delilah's garage and laid a stack of Delilah's mail beside her and happily added "You know what?"

"What?" replied Delilah putting a finishing flourish of eyelashes on the last smiling frog of the day, having no idea how she'd fire them with two non-functioning kilns. She should have bought those kilns half-price when she had the chance but Andrew's pregnant wife frightened her. Those familiar roiling, waves of guilt had splashed over her and off she'd gone, leaving behind the kiln bargain of her whole freaking life.

"Well?" said Joanna, smiling.

"Well?" said Delilah, this memory of humiliation and economic idiocy still fresh.

"Guess what!" said Joanna.

"I'll bite. What?" replied Delilah.

"Janet Simpson refused to fetch coffee for the reptile just as I wouldn't. Just as you ordered me not to, Delilah."

"Excellent," said Delilah still dealing mentally with the possibly terminal consequences of her garage Pottery.

"And Janet Simpson quit!"

"Good for her, love."

"You were right, Delilah! I'm glad I took your advice. I still don't have a job but I am right!"

After Joanna, happy at being right, if jobless, left, Delilah set the finished frogs aside and sat down to read the letters Joanna had brought in for her. The first two were final notices on unpaid bills and the last four were the briefest possible and quite rude rejection letters for all of the stories she had submitted to various publishers. Terribly deflated, Delilah sat and worried until, just outside her garage door a car horn began to toot. But it sounded like the horn on her own old Midget. Pranks! she thought. She would not tolerate pranks today, not even for ready money! She cranked herself up and burst out of her garage primed for an unpleasant confrontation. And here it was! An old MG Midget was being pushed up by an even older man who glared at her and yelled "Where the hell is Jimmy?!"

"I beg your pardon?!" yelled Delilah back.

"That's clear enough, isn't it? Where the fucking hell is Jimmy?" The man stopped pushing and pointed at Jimmy's Auto Repair sign. "Jimmy said he'd fixed this little fucker. For all time, he promised. And now..."

"When?" said Delilah.

"When fucking what?!"

"When the fuck did Jimmy fuck-up your fucking Midget?!" said Delilah not in the mood for pointless vulgarity either, unless it was her own. When needed, she had a fully adequate vocabulary straight from her deceased boxer dad's work-out sessions. "So," she repeated, "when did this alleged repair job occur?"

"A few fucking years ago! Now here I am again. Where the fuck is Jimmy? Are you his latest squeeze, honey? And you should mind your tongue, love. Too many fucks aren't fittin' for a fucking female!"

"What are you, mister, a fucking little old lady who can't hold her own with a full-blown fucking woman?!"

"Where the fuck is Jimmy, love?" he said, simmering down quickly as she seemed to be masterfully calling his bluff.

"Jimmy's fucking dead, you fucking Yobbo sonofabitch!"

"Dead?" said the older man, "Jimmy's dead?"

He suddenly withered, it seemed, to half his size, slumped against the bonnet of his little MG Midget and began to cry like a baby.

"Hell's dangling ballocks," said Delilah after a moment, "What were you? Jimmy's freaking boyfriend?"

"Yeah," he said, wiping his eyes with a grimy hanky, "I was Jimmy's freaking boyfriend ...once. What's it to you, anyhow? You, you cow."

"So, err... Jimmy went both ways, did he?" said Delilah, terribly insensitively, thought Delilah, but this man's overly vulgar language had annoyed her.

"Jimmy went lots of ways and he always came back to me. But that part of it was a long time ago. Years ago."

"And you didn't even know he was gone?"

"He had this new girlfriend, a series of them in fact. I didn't much care for her or them. She was nothing like the first one. The first one was lovely. I never kept track of his girlfriends after Phyllis left."

"Phyllis?!"

"Yeah," he said, "she was lovely."

"They put a good luck shilling over the window here. Years ago," said Delilah.

"How did you know?!"

"Phyllis told me," said Delilah. "Did you and Jimmy put a shilling up too?"

"No, he said, "We put up a sixpence. When did Phyllis tell you this?"

"Not so long ago. Did Phyllis know about you and Jimmy?" said Delilah.

"Sure," he said, "She didn't care a damn about it. She said what was Jimmy's and hers stayed that way. What was Jimmy's and mine stayed that way too. Phyllis was ahead of her time. She was lovely. I was sorry when she left him. So was he. How did you meet her? Is she still alive?"

"Very much so." Delilah pointed to the makeshift patched roof of her own Midget. "That's how I met her. She fell through the top trying to reach their lucky shilling."

"That sounds just like something Phyllis would do, fall through the top of a car." He laughed. "Jimmy and me put our sixpence on the ledge over your garage door. This is the first time I've even thought about it for years. Would you mind if I reclaim it?"

"Help yourself," replied Delilah, "but use your own Midget for a ladder."

"I lost touch with Jimmy. But I wasn't going to let him get away with screwing up my Midget."

"Did he actually screw it up?"

"No." He wiped his eyes again, "Jimmy was the only one I could trust with the Midget. He knew what he was doing. I screwed it up myself, got under the bonnet and thought I was Albert Einstein, I guess."

"What's wrong with it?"

He shook his head. "I got it started this morning. It ran okay and I got it just outside your mews before it stopped again but...are you sure about Jimmy? That he's, you know, dead?" He began again to cry softly.

He's not so old either, not much over seventy, thought Delilah. Men are such softies. Or is it just because he's... older? She gulped back her pre-sob snort. "Fancy a cuppa?" she said, her voice breaking. "I'm Delilah."

"Yes please. That's a very pretty name, Delilah," he replied. "From the Bible. Delilah cut Samson's hair. I'm Jasper. That's from the Bible too but I'm no Bible guy."

"Nor am I, Jasper. I'm going to fix us a cuppa. Then I'll fix your car. Sounds like the Distributor. Your contact points need replacing or adjusting." Her voice was breaking again and at the very edge of her pre-sob snort, she disappeared into the house to emote over the electric kettle before Jasper could say *"You'll fix my car?!"* But he said it anyway. It was as well Delilah didn't hear it because it was 'sexist', he thought and continued to cry a bit and to wipe his eyes with a hanky that didn't help at all. He'd discovered that it had a "J" for Jimmy on it. To hell with the car! His trip to the mews today was to see Jimmy again -- it had been far too long. He blew his nose and softly began again to weep.

An hour later, Delilah had scraped and adjusted the contact point's in Jasper's Midget and it was purring like her new cat friend whom she hadn't seen for a while. Always the cat's prerogative. Jasper tried to pay Delilah for her work as they sat over another cuppa and two iced buns Mum had left in her freezer but Delilah refused.

"On your car doors it says 'Jasper Electrics'. Are you still in the electric business?" asked Delilah.

"Not really. Not anymore, but I help out friends once in a while. I owe you. Can I be of use?"

"I'm a potter and both of my kilns have gone haywire. They're electric. Maybe you could have a look?"

Jasper set down his tea, said "sure thing, love. Both of your kilns have gone haywire? At the same time? That's suspicious."

"I thought so too. Suspiciously bad luck. I'm really in a mess. I've got a couple of orders that I haven't been able to fire."

An hour later, two defective master fuses that only an electrician would have known about, were discovered in the kilns. Then, a quick ride in Delilah's Midget to buy replacements, and both kilns were running beautifully and many smiling ceramic frogs were, with Jasper's help and to Delilah's joy, now being baked to perfection. "You're an Angel, Jasper!" she said, setting out another tea tray -- she'd found two more iced buns in the freezer.

Delilah and Jasper made a deal. He promised to do all her new electrical wiring and had some ideas for a speaker system throughout her house and a new cable set-up to stand ready and easily willing whenever Delilah deigned, as she described it, to again join cyberspace. Jasper had inherited most of the equipment from an office building he'd worked on that was already being razed to be replaced by a skyscraper. Delilah could have the equipment, plus his work for nothing. He was grateful to do something, he said, as a memorial for his beloved Jimmy. In return, Delilah promised him all the vases and ceramic pigs and smiling frogs he'd ever need. She would also see to the ongoing repair of his Midget, assuring him that their two Midgets could live as cheaply as one.

Delilah planned to get Jasper together with Phyllis one day soon but wasn't sure when, so she didn't mention it to Jasper. Though, as he was leaving she did ask him why he had been so fucking vulgar and angry when they first met. It was a front, he assured her. Made him seem a bit dangerous. In the world he knew, it was a plus. Kept him out of most trouble and occasionally, even at his age, had made a few very desirable friends. But it was all a game wasn't it? Delilah agreed it was. A man's game.

"A woman's game too, love," reminded Jasper with a grin as he drove away in his purring Midget which Delilah saw had a spanking new top on it and, luckily, no Phyllis to destroy it. Yet.

With her two kilns operating at full capacity again, Delilah had a lot of catching up to do and her literary adventure was abruptly suspended. Everything she had written had been rudely rejected and she'd totally lost faith in her totally new direction as well as the taste-level of the whole freaking smut industry. Her message to them: Fuck *you*!

Succinctly put, she'd struck out. The Erotic, or at least writing about it, wasn't her cuppa.

But everything else seemed to be on fast-forward. Joanna got an excellent job with a lot of responsibility and, of course, not as much money as a man might have accrued from this same position. Darren had begun behaving himself and was not deserting Joanna twice a week anymore -- or even once a month. Not since she'd got her new job and he was still looking for his. Nigel had gone on holiday and taken his foul mutt with him and Phyllis had been happy to be invited to Delilah's, and after all these years to meet Jasper again. Delilah also got an order for smiling frogs which got her out of the red for a month and enabled her to buy the exact number of remaining bricks she'd need for her brick wall, according to Darren's gift, 'Masonry for Idiots' or was it 'Dummies'?

Darren was now handling all kitchen duties at Joanna's and proved to be an excellent cook as well. His secret part-time kitchen experience had been valuable. This currently content next-door couple were thinking about forming a catering business together and had asked Delilah, entrepreneur that she was, to join them. Delilah's woman within, of course, instantly refused. She had enough on her plate but was happy that Joanna was doing so well.

Phyllis knocked at Delilah's door. She had a bottle of champagne on one arm and in her designer bag on the other was her emergency kit, a large silver flask of Johnny Walker Blue, her favourite scotch. She hadn't had a drink for some time but she felt safer knowing that rescue remained an arm's length away. Though she was cold sober and a bit cranky, Phyllis knew that she was welcome here and Delilah opened the door, pulled her in and hugged her. They were new but firm friends and Delilah had never lifted a finger to 'save' Phyllis from herself. Phyllis was comfortable with this and liked Delilah for it. In fact, felt closer to Delilah because of it, and Jimmy seemed still around the mews too. What one saw in Phyllis was what one got. For good or ill. Delilah never minded a little, or a lot, of either. It was as it was. To be honest, she thought, that should apply to everybody, including Mum. She loved her mother and knew it was mutual. But to each other they remained a large handful. Delilah would work on it, was working on it.

Jasper arrived not long after Phyllis. He'd baked small cakes for both women.

"Jee-sus!" cried Phyllis, "Jee-sus! you don't look a day over eighty!"

Jasper laughed, and said matter-of-factly he wasn't anywhere near eighty and handed the cakes to Delilah and shook Phyllis's hand as she added, "Darling, I should have said what I really thought. That it's wonderful to see you again."

"And I should have said that here is, still is, the loveliest lady I ever met." Jasper looked about to cry but hadn't the chance because Phyllis leaped on him and hugged him.

They sat for an hour during which it was Jimmy this, Jimmy that, and Jimmy emerged as a person Delilah felt might have been her friend, or even lover, had their ages been less disparate. He was, obviously, multi-universally sexy.

Somewhat later, after Phyllis and Jasper had gone, Delilah was in a crushingly sentimental mood brought on by all that talk about Jimmy and lost love. And the champagne, of course. She'd had most of it and it always made her either ridiculously happy or morbidly sad when there was a reason to be sad. There was. She had no idea how she'd pay an immense mews improvement assessment she'd received that morning. She was doomed. Even the bit she had set-by was dwarfed by the unexpected sum.

So Delilah, a huge pickle jar of champagne in hand, was making the most of a sudden case of uncharacteristic self-pity as she wandered through parts of Jimmy's garage she had never explored in the year she'd lived in his mews. Her new life was sputtering to an ignominious end. Would she end up in a one room flat? Or be forced to live with Mum? Not that there was anything wrong with that. But there *was*!

Through a gaping crack in the subsiding back wall of her garage Delilah could see a vast overgrown plot of neglected land, an almost-jungle that seemed forgotten by the world. She'd fix that crack and all the other cracks in the walls when her ship came in! Stop fooling yourself, honey, whispered the woman within as gently as possible and Delilah knew then that her ship would never arrive. It was her shipwreck she was waiting for. Tattered, tired and plaster-dusty, Delilah of the mews knew she was finished. Failure was written across her forehead. She was a phenomenal failure!

Delilah sprawled on the wooden three-legged stool, one of the few practical amenities that came with Jimmy's garage. Bluer than blue, she quaffed the rest of her champagne, squatted there sodden in melancholy and sang miserably, making it up as she went:

"I got the doggone... boo-hoo blues...
Got nothin' more to... lose...
Got nothin' left to... pawn...
Life's a bitch... got a itch to move on...
I got the doggone boo-hoo blues"

Delilah decided instantly that her wretched blues lyrics were no better than her vintage erotica smut and her tears came suddenly, without the decency of a pre-sob snort. Almost immediately, it began to rain, pounding thunderously on the garage's tin roof.

"Shit!" she groaned, "shit! shit! shit!" and wiped her eyes on her sleeve and rushed about placing ceramic bowls in their usual strategic positions to catch the leaks. There were many. Leaks that would never be repaired by her, she who knew how to properly hold a hammer and pound a nail. Who would live here when she was exiled by her poverty? She dropped herself on the wooden stool again and grieved tipsily, audibly, for her dear, derelict relic of a home that might soon be razed never to rise again.

Then Delilah saw, tucked into a crevice, the shiny corner of a small brass box she had never noticed before. A new torrent of rain coursing down over the ragged bricks had washed and revealed it, half-hidden, in the wall. She pulled the box from its watery niche, wiped it with a pottery rag, opened it, and changed her life.

A week later a huge land extension was officially attached to Delilah's deed. This, Delilah confirmed through her solicitor -- an ultra-efficient woman, naturally -- who'd had it verified and recorded.

The metal box contained a signed and stamped ownership transfer of a land extension to be added to Jimmy's deed. It was a gift to Jimmy for many years of unpaid repair on a very old neighbour's lorry. The grateful old man, owner of the sweetshop that was now some posh stiff's pied-à-terre, had made the transfer long before he died but it was not officially recorded because Jimmy, not sure what it actually was, had never got around to it. Jimmy had enough on his plate with auto repair, and women, and men. This considerable plot of land consisted of the vast overgrown garden behind Delilah's little house and garage, the very forgotten jungle she had peered at through that gaping crack and the miserable rubble of her new, single life.

Delilah's broken-down stable, this previously impossible to expand, tiny hut, had now become, even in its devout dereliction, as pricey a plum as might be found in central London. Thus, was Delilah assured by her estate agent, also a woman, who suggested she build a splendid, full size house in the place of her shabby hundred year old stable.

But Delilah's woman within resisted this grandiose plan and insisted that Delilah simply triple the size of her original lot and sell off the rest of the immense jungle-garden. The considerable sum from this sale would add a veritable fortune to her nearly nonexistent bank account, plus easily accomplish the more modest improvements she had in mind.

Jimmy's garage would be extended into a proper pottery, with living quarters above where she'd add a spare bedroom for Mum's overnights or whatever, and possibly a small, centrally located business location for Jasper. After all, it was a semi-commercial mews to begin with and this semi-retired handyman could be relied upon not to demand sex for every small service he provided! It would be pleasant to occasionally have this man around the house. And other men, of course, when the need arose. And it would.

Joanna and Darren were welcome to use, rent-free, a part of Delilah's new, extended pottery building as a super-kitchen for their catering service. Totally convenient, thought Delilah, when lunchtimes rolled around. She, herself, had never felt completely at ease stirring a pot. Tea was her outside limit. Oh, yes! Full speed ahead on her brick wall. And removal of the three implacable prematurely hardened cement sacks. Also, this was crucial, a new top for her Midget. Immediately. And so it was.

Now, after a productive morning in the pottery, Delilah, overflowing still with the Miracle of the past few weeks, plodded from her still primitive garage pottery into her *hut*, through her pretend hall and up the makeshift, ladder-like staircase into the pretend makeshift bathroom and shook off the plaster dust and dried clay and took a bath and dried herself fluffily with a one hundred percent newly purchased, plaster-dust-free towel and found suitable lingerie and a fine silk blouse at the bottom of a box and her black leather jacket on a nail and her best pair of faded jeans on a nail and tore another nice Marks and Sparks cashmere pullover on a nail and sat on her bed cursing happily as she slipped into a pair of sensible shoes, making doubly sure they matched for a change, shoestrings and all, and found a small, empty box and wrapped it from a roll of posh paper requisitioned from a long ago visit to Burberry's.

The wrapped empty box under her arm, Delilah skipped dangerously down her ladder-like staircase and was off to John Lewis's for the whole day, if necessary. What a fine day it was, for an escalator ride or even two or three. And a pint for later, even two or three. In preferred company.

Everything seemed so very much in just the right place now and so was comely Delilah, her feet planted firmly on her favourite highly-polished, department store escalator.

"Modern technology is certainly a marvel" announced Delilah, she, who knew perfectly well what she wanted.

"Yes," added her unique woman within, "isn't it just?!"